David Brooks has published several collections of poetry, short fiction and essays, and three previous novels, *The House of Balthus* (1995), *The Fern Tattoo* (2007), and *The Umbrella Club* (2009). His work has been highly acclaimed, widely translated and anthologised, and shortlisted for the Miles Franklin, New South Wales Premier's, Adelaide Festival and many other awards. In 2011 he published *The Sons of Clovis: Ern Malley, Adoré Floupette, and a secret history of Australian poetry*. He is currently an honorary associate professor at the University of Sydney, where for many years he has taught Australian literature and directed the graduate program in creative writing. A co-editor of the journal *Southerly*, he lives in the Blue Mountains of New South Wales, and spends a small part of each year in a village on the coast of Slovenia.

Also by David Brooks

NOVELS
The House of Balthus
The Fern Tattoo
The Umbrella Club

SHORT FICTION
The Book of Sei and Other Stories
Sheep and the Diva
Black Sea

POETRY
The Cold Front
Walking to Point Clear
Urban Elegies
The Balcony

NON-FICTION
The Necessary Jungle: Literature and excess
De/scription: A Balthus notebook
The Sons of Clovis: Ern Malley, Adoré Floupette,
and a secret history of Australian poetry

TRANSLATION
The Golden Boat: Selected poems of Srečko Kosovel
(with Bert Pribac)

THE CONVERSATION
A TALE

DAVID BROOKS

First published 2012 by University of Queensland Press
PO Box 6042, St Lucia Queensland 4067, Australia
www.uqp.com.au

© David Brooks 2012

This edition published 2013

Design by Sandy Cull, gogoGingko
Cover photographs © iStockphoto; *Still Life with Blue Drapery*
    by Paul Cézanne, c. 1893–94 (oil on paper) © Bridgeman
    Art Library / Getty Images
Typeset in 12/16.5 pt Bembo by Post Pre-press Group, Brisbane
Printed in Australia by McPherson's Printing Group

National Library of Australia cataloguing-in-publication data
is available at http://catalogue.nla.gov.au

The Conversation / David Brooks
ISBN   978 0 7022 4995 2 (pbk)
            978 0 7022 4884 9 (epub)
            978 0 7022 4885 6 (kindle)
            978 0 7022 4883 2 (epdf)

University of Queensland Press uses papers that are natural, renewable
and recyclable products made from wood grown in sustainable forests.
The logging and manufacturing processes conform to the environmental
regulations of the country of origin.

SOCRATES: Dear Phaedrus! Where are you coming from, and where are you going?

PHAEDRUS: I'm coming from Lysias, son of Cephalus, and I am going to take a walk outside the wall.

PLATO, PHAEDRUS

CORNICHE

Why they'd set the meetings up in Monfalcone he couldn't understand. True, it was closer to the site, and they'd put him in a charming hotel on the corniche – a long road virtually at the sea's edge, so gently curved it could almost be straight, right across the top of the Adriatic, all the way to Trieste. But the area appeared empty and spiritless at this time between seasons, not to say windy, and left him with little to do but look inward. No problem normally, he tended to enjoy his own company, but he was in one of those flat places in life, listless.

Perhaps it was just the eight days of negotiations. And the uncertain weather. Some days, advanced as the spring supposedly was – it was the twenty-fourth of May already – seemed to look back toward winter, others only tentatively toward summer, and none of them with much conviction, so that you didn't really know what to do with them. Yesterday morning, from the hotel, he'd watched Robbie, the proprietor of the *trattoria* next door, come out and look at the pale sunshine, roll back his awning with a long crank-handle, then bring just the one table onto the pavement, putting an umbrella into the centre but leaving it furled. An announcement that it was time for the Season to begin. Or perhaps just a plea. As yet, so far as he could tell, no one had sat down there. Maybe today Robbie'd be luckier. It was warmer, the warmest day so far. Emilio at Reception was saying that it was going to be the first real day of summer, twenty-six degrees. The first real day of summer: when was that? The solstice? Weeks away.

No doubt his hosts would have flown him out, as he'd initially requested, immediately after the last meeting, but the flights at that time were wrong. Genevieve and Marina were away for another three days. They'd carefully arranged it so that their absences from Paris would very nearly coincide. He'd rather an extra day or two here than four hours between planes at the airport in Frankfurt – a ridiculous routing, thanks to an industrial dispute – and then arrival at an empty apartment. There would be a direct flight to Orly only on Tuesday. Now, resigned to it, he was glad of a little time to himself. Or imagined that he should be. These things were sent to you, Genevieve would have said, and perhaps you need to look around for the reason. Otherwise he'd never really take time off.

Through the trees over the road the beach was empty except for a couple of meandering dog-walkers. But the sun was out, and strengthening, and the bright blue flag of the region, with its golden eagle, was flapping enthusiastically from the pole by the hotel entrance. The long, straight road, like something out of a movie, seemed to be inviting him. Grace Kelly, he suddenly remembered, and Cary Grant, *To Catch a Thief*. Somewhere on this kind of coast. Monaco.

He might have gone to Venice by train, or rented a car, or asked one of his hosts to drive him, but there would have been too little time; he would have been too rushed. The crowds there, at any time of year. The assault on the senses. What he wanted to do was to think, on his feet, about anything other than the project, or even better

(Genevieve again) not to think at all. Distraction. Enjoy what was turning out to be, just might be, an unusually warm spring day, in a city he'd never been to. Walk among old stone buildings, along cobbled streets. Eat a quiet meal somewhere. Drink – the inspiration had suddenly come to him – a bottle of extremely fine wine (what was the one that Michael had brought him, *Amarone*?). And buy some postcards, send them to the children. No point in sending another to Genevieve and Marina since he'd be back before it arrived, though he could take them some, to give them an idea. No photographs of his own. He hated cameras, carrying them, the way they marked you out. Tourist.

He had declined, graciously, Bartoloni's offer of a lift into Trieste, for fear that it would become a day chaperoned, whether he liked it or not, following a schedule not his own, and had taken a taxi instead. It was a trip of twenty kilometres, and costly, but a beautiful drive, sometimes right on the cliff's edge, high over the sea, sometimes so close to the water it seemed they were driving by a long, concrete beach, sometimes through avenues of trees, tunnels, patches of forest, or large harbour-side parks whose tall, straight tree-trunks reminded him of, who was it? Magritte? Yachts – or their owners – were taking advantage of the wind and sunshine to sketch great arcs and chase-lines on the bright water, stirring within him an old longing. His father. A big sloop, a forty- or fifty-footer, with huge white sails, riding far out, made him ache for Australian water. The Sydney-to-Newcastle. One time only but what a time.

He had been keeping an eye out for the castle, Miramare, that was on so many of the postcards in the hotel foyer, but when he mentioned it the taxi-driver said emphatically that you could not see it from the road, either coming or going, only from the sea. He could have had him take him there – there was a side-road, the driver said, and seemed keen enough to show him – but he sensed the fare would double and he was enjoying, anyway, the wind, and the sun on his arm. If one couldn't see the Castello Miramare from the road then that was it, one couldn't, and he contented himself instead with the thought of the approaching city, coffee in a piazza somewhere, pigeons.

At virtually the first café he saw after he got out of the taxi at the rank beside the railway station, he had ordered a double espresso, asking for extra hot water to tease it out, and a plain croissant, dunking chunks of the pastry in the rich black liquid like a peasant, as Genevieve would have chided, or just an Australian who loved it that way, the oily film it left on the coffee's surface, the delicious confusion of flavours in the mouth, a taste he had always associated with calmness, freedom, sunshine, mornings like this. Strange, how one sometimes knew that one was going to remember something, even as it was happening. The mind running forward, to look back.

He spent what remained of the morning following the ghosts of James Joyce and Italo Svevo through the streets and alleys of the old quarter, guided by a pamphlet handed to him at the Tourist Information Centre. He had devoured Joyce once, *Dubliners*, the *Portrait*, *Ulysses*. He and Carol had had *Pomes Penyeach* beside the bed, in the first years:

> *Around us fear, descending*
> *Darkness of fear above*
> *And in my heart how deep unending*
> *Ache of love!*

He had liked Svevo, too, when at last he'd read him. The *Confessions*. And had always intended to read *As a Man Grows Older*. Perhaps now was the time. He was about to turn fifty-five, after all. Growing older himself. Lines on the face, wrinkled skin on the back of the hands. There was supposed to be a birthday dinner next week, to welcome him home. Some trendy place in Porte de Saint-Cloud, where the price would get in the way of the flavour.

For lunch he had a beer and a sandwich at a café on the waterfront and then spent much of the afternoon wandering about the arcaded shops between the Piazza Unità and the Canal Grande, thinking about gifts, buying some postcards, browsing bookstalls for their English titles (*Antic Hay*, *The Thorn Birds*, *The Turn of the Screw*), avoiding as politely as he could, in one of the darker arches, the offer, in German at first, then broken English, of a Rolex from a black man with rheumy and deeply bloodshot eyes. Eventually, in an up-market boutique, he bought two perfect glass figurines of birds that looked to him like egrets and reminded him of a story Genevieve had told him about her childhood on the marshes in the

Languedoc. He had lingered over the purchase and was about to decide against it for fear that they would break as he carried them about the city through the afternoon or in his luggage later, but the woman in the shop had come over to him and spoken in English – with no hesitation: how could they tell? was it so obvious? – about how beautiful these birds were and, well, he was often trapped like that. She had packed them carefully in a small but sturdy box, and it had fit snugly enough in the pocket of his jacket, which in truth he probably needn't have brought with him in the first place, since he'd spent most of the day so far with it slung over his arm, the sun by mid-afternoon so warm he was choosing the shaded side of the streets, favouring the arcades.

Leaving the shop he was approached again by the man with the Rolex, who seemed to have no sense that he had already approached him scarcely twenty minutes before. This time, with more presence of mind, he smiled and held up his wrist to show that he was already wearing a fake, then reached into his pocket, took out what coins he had, six, seven euros, and gave them to him, gesturing to his eyes, telling him that he should see a

doctor. The nod the man gave made him feel foolish, condescending, barbaric somehow, as if he'd
just tried to say something in a language of which
he had no idea.

He walked off frustrated, thrown. He would
have liked company, after all. Perhaps that's what
it was. But not Bartoloni's. The warm touch
of the voice of the woman in the boutique had
stirred him. Twelve days away from Genevieve
with only the project to talk about, hungry for
the calm of her, and now, with time to himself
and a place that seemed ready enough to welcome
him, he felt locked inside his own language, or
out of it. Strange that he had French down pat
but had never picked up much Italian. Enough to
make his way through a restaurant meal and ask
directions, but little more. Always awkward with
it. Some blockage there. A matter of use. *Dis*use.
The conversation going on inside him with no
easy way out. Which restaurant to choose. What
to look for on these menus. How huge this Piazza
Unità was, its grandeur, opening out on that wide
view of the sea. How strange these tight little
streets and alleys beside it. Lanes full of antique
bookstores, vellum-bound volumes in the musty

windows, sale tables outside, one of them a nest for a large white cat, black collar, lifting its neck to be stroked. Yes. There. A raspy lick of thanks. Deep rumbling purr. The James Joyce Hotel down in that dark alley, the smell of urine, trickle of slimy water into the drain. Would Joyce ever have stayed there? Probably. The sun so strong and yellow in the street beside it. Strong sun, strong shadow. A bright poster on the wall by the door of a music shop. An opera. *Fedra*. In the Piazza Unità in June. That would be something, on a warm summer night, voices soaring and twining in the darkness. A woman looking anguished. Pleading. A young man spurning her. His face a little like Simon's. All the old agonies of love.

Imagining the meal beforehand – he had done this on and off for several days now – he had seen himself sitting outside, in the last of the sunset and into the early dark, and as he strolled down the eastern side of the canal he lingered over the menus of whatever cafés and restaurants had set up tables outside to take advantage of what might become a beautiful evening. Antipasto, pasta, a main course, no dessert but perhaps cheese, gorgonzola by pref- erence. The meal had begun to form itself. He found himself looking for tagliatelle with squid in its own ink. Eaten once, on his first visit to Venice, but never again since. And now it was a hankering. Surely not hard to satisfy since Venice was so close. Supposedly, on a very clear day, you could see it across the water. Or think you saw it. That, or pasta with some of the *tartufi* that Bartoloni had told him time and again were one of the secrets of the region. White truffles. Shaved generously on top, 'making sure', Bartoloni had emphasised, but how did one make sure? 'that they don't use too much garlic, because, to a *tourist*, it *looks* like truffle'. And then seafood – scampi or octopus. This was Trieste after all.

But on the Canal Grande nothing. The bills of fare teased, offered one thing or the other, but not quite enough to make the decision for him. The strongest possibility, food-wise, had the least promising wine list. He found himself entering the Piazza Unità again, just as a cloud that had been masking the sun withdrew, lifting the eastern half of the wide, open space into a warm, deep-yellow glow, a panorama of pigeons and fountain, waiters and umbrellas and glistening glasses.

After a twenty-minute circumnavigation the

prospect seemed clearer. There was a restaurant there, on the north-eastern corner, the Caffè Cosini, marked out by waist-high canvas partitions, with umbrellas up over a dozen starched white tablecloths and an as yet dimly lit but inviting interior. A motif of apples on its crest. Boasting – if he interpreted the Italian correctly – the best of local produce and dishes of the region. An award for the same. A waiter was already lighting tea-candles inside small glass cubes on each of the tables – a little early, perhaps, but it was almost six-thirty, and it might be too late to do so once customers started to arrive. Daylight saving. Glow from the candles would grow stronger as the sun set, continuity between parts of the day, stages of the light, a nice effect. The breeze a little blustery but that might calm.

Enjoying a kind of relief at the decision having thus apparently almost made itself, he walked down the shadowed side of the square, crossed the main road to the harbour's edge, sat at a bench a few minutes looking at the small boats moored there, dinghies and motor-launches, their nets and tackle, observing the intermingling of pigeons and seagulls, enjoying the briny smell and the surprising clarity of the shallow water, low tide by the looks of it. Octopus there, was it? so timid, and such extraordinary camouflage. A pity to eat it. And all these small fishes, what were they? Whitebait? Delicious, but still, a pity, small lives just starting. Nibbling at something floating in the water. A piece of bread. And something else, niggling, at the edge of his mind. The twenty-fourth. An anniversary. His mother's death. How could he not have remembered until now? Ah well, so long ago. Dates a blur sometimes. Sign that life is continuing. One is allowed to forget occasionally.

He stood up again, re-crossed the road and walked up the sunset-lit flank of the piazza toward the restaurant, having resolved, if its menu didn't suit him, to abandon this plan entirely and go back to the piazza where the taxi had dropped him and he had seen a small trattoria with a particular *chianti riserva* that he was curious to try. But it was all there, the squid, the gorgonzola, *tartufi*, and a dozen interesting wines to choose from. No sign of the blustery breeze. Already three of the outdoor tables were occupied, and another had a small *Riservato* sign at its centre. An elegant and slightly nervous middle-aged couple sat at a large table indoors, looking about for the rest of their company, some of whom they must not have known, since they eyed him curiously as he waited to catch the waiter's eye – was he the proprietor? – and be given a place. A moment's fumbling when the waiter approached him in Italian, albeit to switch graciously and immediately into English.

He was offered his choice, and took, outside, the table that seemed most likely to get the last of the sun, and the seat looking down the square toward the harbour. He asked for some bread and mineral water, the wine list, and settled down with the menu. It was entirely in Italian, giving the sense, probably quite false, that this wasn't as tourist-oriented a restaurant as most. And there they all were, pastas and risottos *con tartufi*, three, four, five of them, and sardines, and the squid, the attraction of which paled, suddenly, in the memory of Paul Worthington ordering it in a restaurant in the fifteenth, off rue de Vaugirard, one of those alleys near the old abattoirs, how the sauce had literally blackened his teeth, his lips, so that it had been hard to take his eyes from Paul's mouth, looking as it did like something from *Nosferatu*. Probably not the look after all, for an elegant evening dining in the Piazza Unità.

The waiter arrived with a small basket of rolls, a generous dish of large green olives, and a *Lista dei Vini*, and returned again a few minutes afterward with the water and a blackboard upon which were chalked the day's specials, leaving it propped against a neighbouring table so that signore could study it at his leisure. Apparently – hopefully – it was not one of those places that rushed one. *Insalata al tartufo con asparaghi selvatici.* What was that? Asparagus, yes, and with truffles, but *selvatici*? And *Fiori di zucchina fritti*. Fried zucchini flowers? *Polenta con funghi e pepperoncino. Filetti di sarde al forno*. No, the glassy eyes staring up at him. Accusing. Not tonight. *Stracceti di filetto alla rucola. Strozzapreti con tartufi.*

On the white wine list he found a *Lacryma Christi del Vesuvio*. The name rang a bell. He remembered, after a few seconds, the dinner he had had with Jack Harmon, his father's best friend, four or five years after his father's death, and the vivid ten-minute description – amazing, the memory of the elderly – of a meal they'd had together, Jack and his father, outside Naples in the late 1950s when they were both juniors in the Department of Foreign Affairs. They had drunk

Lacryma Christi, copiously, in a cantina within sight of the volcano. Where had his mother been? Somewhere off with him and his brother, probably, the toddlers. His sister not born yet. Only him and Chris at that point. Jack said that at the time it seemed as if there had been no better wine ever made. Australian ex-servicemen after the War, on their first civilian jaunt overseas. Quite a surprise after Barossa Pearl.

There wasn't much choice: the rest of the wine list had become virtually invisible. He almost snatched at the waiter's arm as he passed – probably not the right thing to do (Genevieve would have chided him for this, too, but only afterward; her gauche Australian, her *gaucho*). But the waiter was friendly and unfazed. Asked which of the day's specials would go best with the wine, he recommended, unreservedly, the zucchini flowers. They come, they go, the waiter said: you must catch them when you see them. There is always pasta, always seafood, but zucchini flowers, fresh like these? hardly ever at this time of year, so early, the first. He ordered them, said that he was very tempted, then, by something with truffles, but needed an explanation of *strozzapreti*.

The waiter smiled. '*Strozzapreti*? Is a kind of hand-rolled pasta,' he said, 'from Romagna, but one of our chefs is very good making them. They are shaped like the little cigarettes you roll for yourself, between the 'ands,' making a gesture most unlike rolling a cigarette, 'and they take the *tartufi* very well. *Strozzapreti* means "to strangle the priest".'

'"To strangle the priest"?'

'Yes,' he said, smiling suddenly. 'Is very popular pasta in Trieste!'

'Okay then. I'll have that too. How will it go with the *Lacryma Christi*?'

'Not as well as a red wine from the Carso, I think, a *refosco*, but still good. In Napoli they would probably have *Lacryma Christi* with their *tartufi*, if they have *tartufi* there, but I think maybe they don't. We have the best *tartufi* here, *tartufi bianchi*, from up in the hills.

'And *secondo*?' The waiter seemed to want something else.

'*Secondo*?'

'Yes, for after the *strozzapreti*. Some fish perhaps?'

'I don't know.' Thinking of the octopus, *Nosferatu*. 'How large are your servings, of the *strozzapreti*?' He was beginning to fear that his elegant night might turn into something gargantuan.

'It depends. We can do them small, or larger, for a main meal.'

'Well, perhaps you could do mine somewhere in between. I am hungry, but my appetite is not what it once was.' He wanted to be sure that there was room for gorgonzola.

'Certainly.'

She came about five minutes later and sat at a table opposite him and closer to the wall, her back to the sea. Slim, not particularly tall, auburn hair, close-cropped, rather more studious than beautiful. Strong-featured. Or was it sharp-featured? A blend. In black jeans, a black jacket. Silver bracelet on a slender wrist. He might not have noticed so much had not the waiter, like a moth to a flame, come so quickly from inside and been so attentive to her. Or had she not, having spoken so fluently with the waiter in Italian – a beautiful voice, unexpectedly calm and gentle, contralto – taken from her shoulder-bag a novel in English, *Possession*, and begun to read. Large, dark eyes, a little like Genevieve's; firm, slim hands.

He realised with some embarrassment that he had been staring, or doing something very much like it, and hoped that no one had noticed, though he thought better of looking around to see. Had she sensed it? Genevieve had told him that women don't have to make eye contact to know when they are being watched. With relief, he remembered his postcards, took them out of his jacket pocket. Different views of the Castello Miramare. One each to his son and daughter, in New York and Sydney respectively, whom he'd not seen since last Christmas and would be unlikely to see again together until the next. He enjoyed the thought of surprising them with a postcard from the Adriatic, just as they were starting to think it their prerogative to surprise him with reports from their own exotic places. The Maldives. Belize. Vietnam. This had been his first job out of France for a while. The problem of becoming too senior in the firm. Thank goodness for the occasional multinational syndicate.

CAFFÈ COSINI

ANTIPASTO

He had written to Simon and was halfway through a card to Anne when, simultaneously, the waiter arrived with his wine and a gust of wind came out of nowhere and, as if singling him out, caught the open umbrella above his table and sent his bread and his postcards flying and the blackboard of daily specials smacking loudly to the ground. In his attempt to catch his postcards, he or the wind, it was not clear which, caught also the small glass cube and the tea-candle, sending them crashing to the stone paving of the square. A small squall of confused apologies followed, from both him and the waiter, who placed the wine and the last of the olives on the neighbouring table while – although the wind, bizarrely, seemed to have disappeared as quickly as it had come – he took down the umbrella and went inside for a broom and a fresh tea-candle. He had barely settled and begun to look for his postcards when the young woman caught his eye and held them up to him. They each rose, he stepping carefully over the broken glass to go over to get them, and she to bring them to him, and, catching themselves doing this, each smiled broadly. When he reached her – she had sat down again – she asked him whether he would like to join her.

'It will give the waiter a chance to clear away the glass, and the wind is quite settled' – this in perfect English, with almost no trace of accent. 'I don't think it will trouble us again, but if it should do so this table is more protected, and the two of us should be able to keep it in place.'

He accepted at once: there seemed no reason not to, though he pretended to make it a condition that she share his wine.

'With pleasure!' she responded. 'What wine have you ordered?'

He went back for the bottle and, once more skirting the broken glass, moved to her table. She smiled again, as if this arrangement pleased her, told him straight out, as a conversation opener, that his *Lacryma Christi* would be excellent for the zucchini flowers, but asked him if it wasn't perhaps a little too gentle for the *tartufi* and the strangled priests.

'The pasta? How did you know?'

'I asked the waiter about you. He didn't know anything, only that you were some kind of English, so I asked what you had ordered. I thought that maybe I could tell something from that.'

'"Some kind of English". I like that!' The Australian in him rankling. 'Do you do this often?'

'What? Question the waiter? Only when something interests me. I like to look at people and guess what I can about them. I don't often like to talk with them. But you seemed harmless enough.'

'Harmless? Should I take that as a compliment?'

'Anyway you like. But, as I imagine them, the most dangerous men don't write postcards.'

'As you imagine them . . . But perhaps we do it as cover.' Genevieve would have said that he was flirting, but wasn't it just banter, good humour? Already he sensed that this young woman had a sense of irony, recognised at least some of the quotation-marks. 'But what was that that you were saying about the wine?'

27

'Only that the white wine – and it's a little sweet, isn't it, the *Lacryma Christi*? as well as sentimental? – might be too soft, *dolce*, for the *tartufi*. And it's not from this region. Perhaps a local white wine would be better, a *malvasia*, or a *friulano* from the Isonzo, or a red wine, a *teran*, from the hills behind us here.'

'Sentimental? What do you mean?' The waiter, by this time, had returned with a brush and pan and a replacement candle-holder, and was sweeping up the broken glass.

'Only that it is a lovely name. Who could resist drinking the tears of Christ?'

'And *teran*?'

'Yes, from the *Carso*, the Karst, up behind us. Made from *refosco* grapes. A very dry red wine, very – I don't know how to say it – *stony*: can you say "stony" about a wine? It is all limestone around here. Many caves. But maybe it would be too harsh, too dry. Too acidic. There is a story that James Joyce thought it the perfect wine to serve to one's enemies.'

'First harmless and now an enemy!' He smiled again. 'But yes, I do like stony red wines. Or flinty: we would probably call them *flinty*.'

'Ah yes, well, the *teran* is good. You will like it, I think. It must be much better now than it was when James Joyce lived here. It has the richest colour. And – how do you say it – it *grows* on you. You should not leave Trieste without trying it.'

'Very well, I will have a glass with my truffles, on your recommendation, but only if you have one too. You seem to know the area well. Do you live here? You're not a native . . .'

'Why do you think that?'

'I don't know. Jumping to conclusions. It occurred to me, just then, that someone who had lived here all their life was not so likely to be dining alone.'

'Well, in fact I did not plan to eat alone. I was to be here with a friend but she could not come. But yes, you are right, I used to live here, though not for all my life. And I don't any more. I was here three years ago, for ten months only, my first job, but now I live in Torino.'

'Torino? So you *are* Italian. I was wondering. You speak such good English. But you also spoke Italian, to the waiter, so fluently. And you are reading Byatt.'

'Yes, Torino, but I am not from there either.

I am actually from the Veneto, from a small village near a small town near Padua. And yes, I speak Italian, of course, and English, and French, and Russian too. I am a linguist, an interpreter with one of the car companies, but in fact I also freelance. I do translation, for example, for a publisher. I like to read English novels from time to time.'

'Books? Do you translate books?'

'Yes, but technical, not literary. And documents, contracts, manuals for electronic devices, things like that. I would prefer to translate novels, but there is no money in that. What do you do?'

'I am an electrical engineer. But a well-read engineer,' blushing suddenly, but he had felt that he should say that, 'since my wife owns a bookstore. I've been in Monfalcone for a set of planning meetings for a new medical centre.'

'Medical centre! Excellent!'

'Yes, a very large one, and quite complicated, from a planning perspective, since it involves so many facilities. It's an international project. There's a lot of French money in it, and a lot of Austrian.'

'But what kind of English are you? You are from England, yes?'

'No. I'm Australian. But I live in France now, in Paris – have been there for almost twenty years.'

'Paris? From Australia? How did that happen? Why would you live in France if you could live in Australia? Such an amazing place, I think. I would love to visit Australia. The reefs – I have seen movies of the reefs! – and the animals! You have such lovely animals!'

'It's not so strange. My mother was part French, although not from France but from the New Hebrides. I got interested in French literature in high school. I even had six months in Canada on an exchange scholarship, at a high school in Quebec. And I studied it all the way through university.'

'Along with electrical engineering.'

'Along with electrical engineering, yes, although I think my heart has always been divided. I had also wanted to study literature. And after I'd worked in Australia for a while a company I had been seconded to needed someone for a French project and I went to Lyon for a year. Then I moved to a French company, and I have been in France ever since.'

'So is your family French or Australian?'

'Family?'

'Yes. The postcard, to your son. I didn't read it, I promise – your handwriting is terrible! – but I did see that part. "My dear son".'

'My children stayed with their mother in Australia for the first ten years or so after she and I divorced, but they had been in Paris as very young children. I would see them a lot even in Australia. After a year or two it was not very acrimonious. You eventually become rather embarrassed about all that, I think. Certainly we did. And then first one child and then the other felt the lure of Paris again. My son came over and worked there for a while, and lived with us – my new wife and me – and my daughter has gone back and forth like a yo-yo, as they say,' hoping that 'yo-yo' might mean the same to an Italian as to an Australian. Apparently it did.

They had each finished a glass of the *Lacryma Christi* and he took a moment to pour another, surprised at how clear it was, how colourless, like water, but with such intensity of flavour, flowers, herbs, the *alcools*.

❧

Before they could resume their conversation the waiter arrived with their first courses, the zucchini flowers for him and a small plate of what looked to be very slender asparagus on a bed of dark, delicate greens for her.

Marvelling at the zucchini flowers – their golden yellow, veined with green, caught, as if in some ethereal amber, in a batter so thin it might better have been called a glaze – and looking up, afraid that he might have been rude, somehow, in his distraction, he found her watching his reaction with clear, shared delight.

'It is not often, to find them like that,' she said, 'fried so simply, and so beautifully. Normally they are stuffed, with ricotta and herbs, or sometimes even with forced meat of some kind. But that seems so *cruel* to them, so brutal, so heavy, to drown out their own flavour with so many others. The simplest method is the best. I have tried often to cook them this way, and have *almost* done it once, but since then, although it seems so uncomplicated, something has always gone wrong. The flour is too crude or the oil is not hot enough. This cook must be very good indeed. Such a delicate touch with the batter.'

'Your English is really very good!' He couldn't help himself, hoped immediately that he hadn't seemed condescending. 'You must have spent a lot of time in England.'

'Not really, no. My mother was an English teacher, like my grandmother before her, so there was a lot of it around me when I was growing up. And I had an English friend, for six months or so, while I was at university. He didn't speak any Italian. He came for a holiday and stayed on. That was even better, I think, than spending the same time in England. We did go to London for a week, as a kind of holiday, but that was all. And I studied English, of course, at high school and university. And now, in my job, I have to speak it a lot. It is, how to put it without irony? the *lingua franca*. Some days I think I speak more English than Italian.'

He suddenly realised that he did not know her name. Somehow they had slipped past the moment when protocol would have determined an exchange, crossed the border without attracting the attention of the guards. But he would go back, now that they had shown that they could do it:

'Stephen Mitchell,' he said, looking her directly in the eye – then, seeing the flash of confusion, extended his hand, smiling. She smiled broadly in return, realising, and extended her own hand above the food. 'Irena,' she said, with an engaging formality: 'my name is Irena Rizzoli. I am pleased to meet you.' Her handshake was firm, strong, and her skin warm and smooth. He wondered, suddenly, what she might think of his. Warm, dry hands, a slight paperiness to the skin, as older people often had, a million fine wrinkles. Would she think him old? Some greying about the temples. Genevieve, kind about it, said that he had a face that spoke of weather and sunshine – that although he had lived in Paris for a long time he had not been *rarefied*.

He relaxed. She returned the conversation to his family and he found himself telling her about the first years in Paris, the children, Carol's return to Sydney, the divorce. The merest sketch only, salted as it was with questions from her about the Australian bush and Australian wines and interspersed by the first delicious morsels of zucchini flower, but he was surprised at how simply and easily it could be told, at such distance, in light of all that had happened since. A third of a lifetime away, almost. Though it seemed still so recent.

Things that had taken him many months to tell Genevieve now told within minutes to a perfect stranger. And yet she, this Irena, had probably only just embarked upon such things, if she had embarked at all. It occurred to him, not for the first time, that she couldn't be much more than Anne's age, if she was that. Twenty-seven? Thirty? But then the young had such energy, and he was forgetting what he himself had been like. Probably she had lived a lifetime already. How many philosophers, writers, mathematicians – electrical engineers – had more great ideas before they were twenty-five than they ever had after.

'Your flowers!' – it startled him, when he might have expected some comment on his story: 'We should not be talking while they sit there cooling. Finish them. I will leave you in peace. It is best to eat them hot. They are such a delicacy, especially when fried like that. I've never seen them look so crisp and delicate, almost Japanese.' When in truth he had already eaten several, and yes, they were very different, a discovery. They reminded him of the first time he'd tasted deep-fried bean curd, a salt crispiness on the outside, watery succulence within. An art, probably, to get the balance right.

He asked about her asparagus, and the meaning of *selvatici* – 'wild', apparently, with a gentle correction of his pronunciation. She seemed to pick up with the change of subject. Not markedly – she'd appeared interested enough – but her face, her eyes had been searching.

'Wild asparagus,' she told him, 'grows all over this area. In the lanes and the forests, and beside the fields. On long stalks, almost up to your waist. It grows in the Veneto, too, where I come from, but not as plentiful or delicious as here. We used to go out to pick it when I was a child. I remember the first time I went with my mother. I got so upset that she had gathered a whole handful – all you need for a meal – in the time that it took me to find three stalks. But they were so much like grass! It was so hard to tell what was asparagus and what was not. Later I got much better. It is beautiful in the morning, with scrambled eggs, mixed into them, but also cold in salads, or fried crisply until almost burnt, my favourite way, and then tossed with garlic and olives, baby tomatoes and pepperoncini – chillies – in a pasta. This salad was very good – not as good as I can do, but a nice dressing, good vinegar and excellent oil, and just enough salt, and pepper. I would add a little *salvia.*'

'*Salvia?*'

'Yes, the herb,' then, seeing that he did not recognise it, 'with slightly furry leaves – *velvet* leaves? – and purple flowers.'

'Sage?'

'Yes, yes, that is right, *sage*, not a very common thing to have with asparagus, I imagine, but I like it,' and with a piece of bread she mopped up some of the dressing, heavy with oil, and took it to her mouth thoughtfully, as if she had just been reminded of something. There was a longish pause.

'Russian,' he said at last, 'did you say you speak Russian? How did that come about?'

'My grandfather. A long story.'

'Tell me!' He was suddenly curious, to hear something of this woman's background, having probably bored her already with too much of his own.

'He was a partisan, during the war, fighting in the Alps. And by the time the war ended he was a dedicated communist. He hadn't had much education – the war interrupted that – but he taught himself Russian so that he could read Trotsky and

Lenin in the original. A sort of obsession. It's my mother's father I'm talking about. I grew up in his house. She was an only child and my father was one of several. When they married it made sense for them to live with her family rather than his. And so I grew up in this house filled with volumes of Trotsky and Lenin and Bakunin and Gorky and so many others, all in this mysterious script I couldn't read. When I was eleven my grandfather started to teach me Russian; not very much, the letters and sounds only. He died not long after we began, but it sowed the seed.'

'A partisan! For a while when I was a teenager I couldn't read enough about them. Caught up in the romance, I suppose. The resistance. But it must have been very hard, very dangerous.'

'He was only a teenager himself. Twenty-one when the war finished. It was a miracle that he survived. He and a schoolfriend – how do you put it? "went underground"? – in 1943, after Salo was created – you know about Salo? – and spent the next years in the Alps as part of a brigade sabotaging supply chains. That is how he met my grandmother. She was a young girl in one of the families that had sheltered him, in a remote mountain village. After the war he went back to find her. He borrowed a friend's truck but it broke down and he ended up hitch-hiking most of the way. It took him two days. He liked to remind her that he had had to sleep under a bridge, and nearly froze to death, all for love.'

'Wonderful.'

'Yes, romantic, although it wasn't that simple. She had gone away to study to become a teacher, so she wasn't there! And people joked with him that she had gone off to become an English teacher because of an American soldier she had met during the liberation. My grandfather went away heart-broken. Hitch-hiked all the way home. But word got to her somehow, and about a week after he had got back, thinking he had lost her, she turned up at his door.'

'And never left.'

'Well, no. Actually she left straightaway, to finish her studies, and it was two years before they could marry. At her insistence. My grandfather always brought it out as her greatest stubbornness.'

'Was she a communist too, your grandmother?'

'Yes. But it was my grandfather who was the more driven. He was from a family of wine makers. After the war, with his brothers, he started organising cooperatives of local grape-growers. And in the 1960s he was one of the first communist mayors in our region.'

'Does it run in the family? Are your parents communist too?'

'My parents? No. I think there was a generation gap. And things have changed. My father was a football player, a very promising one when he was young, but he broke his leg badly in a car accident – he loves fast cars – and could not play any more. So he is now a coach, a very good one, of a professional team. Two of his players have played for Italy.'

'Impressive! And you? Are you closer to your father or your grandfather?'

'Closer? Do you mean in beliefs? I don't know. I loved football as a child, and wanted to play it, and I love fast cars, but in beliefs I think I am closer to my grandfather. Perhaps more like he was when I knew him, in his later years, when he was more cautious. He became disillusioned with Stalin in 1956, with the suppression of the Hungarian uprising and all those revelations about Stalin's internal repression, and again in the late '60s with the crushing of the Prague Spring. And then, later, much more, with the Red Brigade. I think they were his final disillusionment. My name is Irena Alda, you know, Irena *Alda* Rizzoli . . .'

She paused, as if he should understand something by that, but then, seeing his confusion, 'Alda, after Aldo Moro.'

'Moro? The Prime Minister who was kidnapped?'

'Yes. He was not Prime Minister any more, when he was kidnapped, but yes. I was born the day after his body was found. A Christian Democrat. My grandfather insisted that I be called Alda in his memory. He had never agreed with Moro's politics but he thought the Red Brigade had gone too far.'

'It must have been difficult for him, all those disillusionments. Hungary. Czechoslovakia. The Red Brigade.'

'Yes, I think so. Very. But he saw them as other people going astray, not as failures of communism itself. That's what the books were about, and his learning Russian. To have the original words, and not to have to rely on other people's interpretations.

'The *teran*,' she announced then, breaking away, as if she had gone farther than she wished, 'let's order the *teran*.' And they had before them, within minutes, a glass each of what the waiter assured them was almost the best in the cellar, and tasted it while waiting for their main course: stony (she had been right) and astringent, hard-won, full-bodied, with a rich, deep colour, a mixture of ruby and something browner, garnet, and a depth and complexity of flavour if, as she instructed him to do, one waited for it behind the first harsh, almost acidic gust. Tannins, he realised: he had never had a wine so tannic. The wine he had wanted, without knowing it. He complimented her on her suggestion, then asked her what had brought her back to Trieste.

'A whim,' she said, and then corrected herself: 'Well, not exactly a whim, since I had been thinking for at least two weeks about going somewhere. I needed to get away, escape for a little while, but I couldn't decide where. I was thinking of places closer to Torino, or of perhaps going home. And then, like an inspiration, I thought of coming here. I called Claudia, the girl I used to share a house with, one of my best friends, and came down to see her. I gave her only sixteen hours' notice. I called her to see if it was alright to come, and then went to bed, and when I got up in the morning I packed and got into the car.'

'And drove across Italy.'

'Yes, and drove across Italy. But that is not a problem. I love driving, especially on the *auto-strada*. And then talked all night.'

'So why are you dining here alone?'

'Well, I am not alone, am I? The wind has helped me with that. A gust of wind and some broken glass. An *accidental* meeting, you might say. But yes, we were supposed to come here together, Claudia and I, but her mother, who now lives with her, was taken ill yesterday – a mild heart-attack, but she will be alright. Claudia has spent the day at the hospital and wants to be there this evening. There has been a steady flow of other relatives and I thought it best to get out of everyone's way. Since I was so looking forward to it – this restaurant – I decided that I would come by myself. I have to be back in Torino on Tuesday so we couldn't have postponed it.'

'Is this restaurant one of your favourites?'

'Yes, though I have not come here very often. Perhaps three or four times. The food is good, very fresh and local, yet sophisticated at the same time, and it is a little *expensive*, like everything else around the piazza. But there are times when it does one good to spend a little money on oneself, knowing that you can't afford it, and that you don't care. And, you know, to have this *grandeur* around you, this big, open space, like a vast empty theatre, when we spend so much of our lives so knotted in tangled little balls of ourselves. Some people don't like it, find it *too* open, but I find that it picks up the spirit. And tonight we are lucky.'

'Lucky?'

'Yes,' she said, with a smile he might have called mischievous, 'you are lucky to have found me, and I am lucky to have found you. We can be company. But I mean also that it is quiet and uncluttered. Often when I have come here, especially when it has been later in the summer, there has been scaffolding and seating for the concerts, or they have been putting it up or taking it down. But this evening it is clean, open.

'There are a lot of concerts here, in the open air. A very popular place for them.'

'I saw a poster for an opera here, in June. *Fedra*.'

'Operas. Yes. They do three or four each summer, for a few nights every month. But there are also other concerts. Leonard Cohen, Ana Gabriel, Tereza. Do you know Tereza?'

'No.'

'*Fado*. She is a singer of *fado*. Do you know *fado*?' She must have been able to read the blankness on his face. 'A Portuguese singing style. Very beautiful. Love songs very often. From the bars of Lisbon. But you know Leonard Cohen?'

'Of course. One of the voices of my youth. And one of Genevieve's favourites, even now.'

They looked, for a moment, around them. The waterless fountain. The vast piazza slipping gradually into dusk. A hundred people wandering about in it making no difference to its apparent emptiness. He could imagine it would seat thousands.

'Do you know anything about it – that opera, *Fedra*?' he asked, having tried to visualise. 'I can't say I've heard of it before.'

'*Fedra*? No. But wouldn't it be *Phaedra*? "P-h-a-e-d-r-a", in your spelling? Based on the play?'

'*Phaedra*? Ah, of course! So *Fedra* is Italian for *Phaedra*? That would explain it, the woman in love with her son. There was a picture on the poster, a young man spurning an older woman, in some sort of horror or alarm.'

'Yes, but I don't think the play is actually called *Phaedra*, at least not the one I'm thinking of, by Euripides. That's called *Hippolytus*, after the boy. And he's her stepson, not her son. A messy play. We did it at university. I didn't like it much.'

'You did it at university? Do you mean you acted in it?'

'No!' She laughed, briefly. 'No. But I studied Classics. English, Russian, Classics, Linguistics. And I wrote an essay once on Euripides. His misogyny. I got quite involved in it.'

'So how is *Hippolytus* a "messy" play?'

'She's tricked into it, Phaedra. It is a spell cast on her by Aphrodite. You don't know this?'

'No. I said "well-read" but there are a thousand gaps.'

'Phaedra is married to Theseus. Theseus has a son, Hippolytus, by an earlier lover – or wife, I don't remember. Hippolytus is young, eighteen or nineteen, something like that. And Aphrodite, the goddess of love, is angry because he will not serve her, but devotes himself instead to Artemis, the goddess of hunting and chastity. In her anger she casts a spell on Phaedra so that she falls in love with him. Phaedra – this is much of the drama, all her torment – struggles against this terrible feeling she suddenly has. For her stepson! She even thinks about killing herself to get rid of it.'

'How does that work? Aphrodite wants to punish Hippolytus, so she torments Phaedra?'

'It's complicated, as I told you, messy. Phaedra is deeply ashamed of her feelings, mortified, and does all she can to prevent Hippolytus from hearing about them. He is very self-righteous and she knows that he'll scorn her horribly if he learns how she feels. Not to mention how her husband Theseus might react, if he were to hear.'

'I still don't get it. It sounds like Phaedra is being punished, not Hippolytus!'

'That's part of the misogyny. The point of the play isn't quite what it seems. Phaedra tries to keep her feelings from Hippolytus, but her nurse tells him anyway, and he acts as you might expect. In fact he delivers a terrible speech against women, calls them noxious weeds, a curse against men. A horrid speech.'

'So where is Aphrodite's revenge in all this?'

'Phaedra kills herself, but she leaves a letter to

Theseus that takes her own revenge by saying that Hippolytus has raped her. And when Theseus gets back – he has been away through all of this – there is a trial and Hippolytus is banished, and Theseus calls upon Poseidon to destroy his son. Hippolytus is travelling along the coast, on his way into exile, and there's a giant wave, a kind of tidal-wave – a very strange moment – and a hideous bull emerges from it, frightening Hippolytus' horses, who drag Hippolytus to his death on the rocks.'

'So Phaedra turns from victim to avenger?'

'Yes, Euripides is painting a rather terrible portrait of women and of love. Maybe that's the real point. Hippolytus ends up a kind of hero.'

'But why the bull? What's that about?'

'I'm not sure. Phaedra was the daughter of Pasiphae and the Minotaur, do you know that story?'

'Yes. The woman who hid inside a wooden cow so that she could experience the sexual power of the Minotaur.'

'Yes, and there's obviously some sort of connection there, but I cannot see what it is.'

'Didn't Theseus slay the Minotaur, on one of his other adventures? Ariadne fell in love with him and showed him how to find his way through the labyrinth, and when he'd slain the Minotaur and come out he took Ariadne with him, but then abandoned her?'

'On Naxos, yes.'

'Yes,' he said. 'On Naxos.' Memories rippling about him.

She took a breath, as if she was about to say something further, but held it, then exhaled slowly, to all appearances relinquishing whatever it was she'd had in mind. He could see this and wondered what it might have been, but said nothing. Instead they looked out again at the great square, upon which, yes, a quite complicated play might be enacted. The waiter, taking advantage of the momentary silence, came over and collected their empty plates, asked if there was anything else they would like, more bread, more water, another glass of the *teran*? Their pastas should not be much longer: that is, if they wished – or he could hold them back, it was up to them. The restaurant was filling up. A fourth and fifth table had been taken outside, and inside was looking busier too. She said something to him in Italian. It seemed a little delay was being arranged: there was no rush.

'Is it work you are escaping from?' he asked her, somehow sensing that it was not. 'It can't be the weather, at this time of year.'

'No, it is not work. The work is fine, in fact easy at the moment, and the weather lately has been getting better every day. It is my own head, I think.'

'Your own head? You can't escape that so read-ily, surely.'

'No, but you can give it a change of place, a change of scenery. I have been trying to sort out a problem and have been getting nowhere . . . You can get boxed into a space and not see your options. I thought that a long drive and a long talk with someone might help me to think more clearly.'

'A problem?' Most of the time people didn't mention problems that they didn't want to talk about. He would normally have skirted the issue – he hadn't come to the restaurant to listen to someone's problems – but he had already told her about his divorce, distant as it was (and his second: he hadn't mentioned the first), and had felt himself inching toward other things, before the bracing astringency of the *teran* had helped him think the better of it. A young woman's problems might be a change from his own concerns, which weren't, these days, to do with anything much more than aging, and deciding on the right time to up-stakes with Genevieve and try some of the things they'd been talking about, while they still could. Go back to Australia. Rent a four-wheel-drive. See the desert. Sleep in the dry bed of a river. And what kind of problems could this young woman have, anyway?

'A problem with a relationship, or perhaps it would be better to say non-relationship.'

'A non-relationship? Is this with the Englishman?'

'No. That was some time ago, and was never very serious. This one feels as if it might be different. It is happening and not happening at the same time; a relationship that has started and yet has never started, that exists and does not exist, simultaneously.'

'It sounds almost like a philosophical problem . . .'

'Perhaps it is, in a way, who knows? I met someone, an older man – not as old as you are (sorry!), but quite a bit older than me nonetheless. Fifteen years older, in his early forties. A Russian. He had come to Torino to work with one of the car companies, on a contract. I know that it sounds strange that Italians might look elsewhere for a designer, but this one is brilliant. He has solved some problems they've been troubled by for years, and they are trying to, what is the word? *poach* him? Though I think also that he is caught up in some larger politics, that the Italian company is actually trying to prepare for a major push into the Russian market. And I was employed as the interpreter. I worked with him for three weeks, and nothing happened, not really, nothing between us. I thought he was nice, attractive, in a bearish kind of way – he is a big man, a strong man – and we had some pleasant conversation.

'He was lonely, missed his wife and his young children, and it was frustrating for him to be able to speak so little Italian, so I think he was grateful for anyone who could speak Russian, and it probably made us seem closer than we would normally have been. I did not even realise that I was beginning to be drawn to him. I was seeing someone else, and had been very close to this other person, and for most of the three weeks was rather preoccupied, emotionally. But in the last few days, while he was busy instructing the Italian designers who were going to be continuing the project with him long-distance, and negotiating with the bosses who were trying to persuade him to stay longer, I caught him, once or twice, looking at me: there was eye contact and it was . . . intense, you know? Intense. I think it surprised both of us. And I should have left it there.'

'But you didn't?'

'No. I did things. Small things. Dressed for him. Tried to look my best. Didn't avoid eye contact. And at the end of his last meeting I drove him back to his hotel. It was on my own way home and I had done this a few times already. He asked me to come to the reception counter with him because he had a problem with his bill that he wanted my help to explain to them. I don't think he had any other intentions. It was a simple problem, easily resolved, and at the end of it we went back outside to the car and said goodbye in the usual way for people who have become friends, you know, a kiss into the air beside the right cheek and then a kiss into the air beside the left, and if you are enthusiastic enough another kiss into the air beside the right cheek again. Only we both stopped in the middle, on the second pass, and there was this brief kiss on the lips. At least, it should have been brief. It was only a touch at first, but I opened my mouth. It was impulsive. I don't know where it came from. Something got into me, a kind of mischief or wickedness, though it didn't feel like that. In a way I didn't even really mean it, at first. But the kiss! the force of it, the openness and depth of it, there in the street! – it shocked us both.'

'And,' trying not to think of her mouth, of such kisses, 'did something else happen?' – not able to help himself – 'Did you . . .'

'No. Nothing else. I don't think either of us knew what to say. Maybe something else *should* have happened. I wish that it had. So that we could deal with it, you see, know what it is. Perhaps it would have put an end to it. But nothing else did happen. I got into my car. It was in front of the hotel and another car had arrived and was waiting behind me, and I felt rushed, and couldn't think. I got in and he bent down and looked at me through the passenger window, only that, looked at me, and then I drove off. And he left the next day. I thought he might call me that night, after the kiss, but he was going out, on his last evening, with some Russian friends, and they kept him late, and when he came back to the hotel – he explained all this to me later – it was very late, and he was a little drunk, and he forced himself not to call, because he felt some sort of disaster would come of it, for me as much as for him.'

'But he contacted you later, obviously.' They had almost finished their glasses of *teran*. Should he order others? or simply revert to the *Lacryma Christi* which was waiting beside them in an ice bucket now trickling with condensation? No. Wait. Pace himself.

'Yes, he did, he sent me a note, to thank me for my help, and I responded, and he wrote again, and then called, or rather called me back when I tried to call him at his business number. And we began to correspond more seriously. By email. It was a little awkward, formal at the beginning. I found myself looking for hints, reading between the lines, testing him with hints of my own.'

'Hints?'

'Yes, signs of affection, moving from "best wishes" to "affectionately" – things like that – to see if he responded in the same way, and he did.

And soon it was "as ever", and we were writing about more and more personal subjects, going from the kinds of things you tell to an acquaintance, to things you tell to a friend, to things you tell to an intimate, to things you tell to almost nobody. It was a bizarre escalation if you look at it from the outside, but it seemed so natural. And soon – within months – there were actual declarations of love; *assumptions*, in a way, to begin with, but then actual declarations. The letters became like diary entries. We started sharing each other's lives. And that is what we are doing, now, and I love him, or think I do.'

'But?'

'Well, it *is* bizarre, surely. I hardly know him, except through the emails, and he hardly knows me. We have not touched each other except for that kiss. I don't even know what prompted that kiss. That is so unlike me. I have never done anything like that before. I am usually so contained, so reserved. This thing has come out of nowhere.'

'Hardly out of nowhere, I would imagine. The desire must come from somewhere, might have been building up, for both of you, for a long time. The kiss was impulsive, yes, and maybe you shouldn't have done it, but who can say, really? Certainly not a stranger like me! We all want someone who can tell us what is right and wrong in situations like that. There have been times in the past when I'd have done almost anything to find someone who could tell me, definitively, whether what I was doing was right or was wrong – but although there are plenty of people who would like to advise us, who is there who really knows?'

'Some people seem to be very clear on such things!'

'Yes, of course. But we all have only the one life, and we all can work only on the evidence that comes our way. Your kiss began something, that much is clear – and it sounds as if it was a wonderful kiss! – but it seems, too, that there was something there to be unlocked in the first place, and the letters and emails did the rest, as they will do, following a logic of their own, especially with someone you hardly know.'

He paused there, needing to take a breath. She was looking down at her plate. He couldn't read her face. Probably he had said too much. He apologised. Said he must be boring her, that this probably wasn't the kind of response she'd been seeking.

'No!' she said. 'Not at all. But explain to me more, please, about letters having a "logic of their own".'

'Letters go into open space – I don't know what else to call it – and they are read in it, almost as if they *come* from it. The lack of knowledge on both sides creates a kind of vacuum, though it's actually more like a field of potential.'

'A field of potential?' She smiled. 'That sounds like a term from electrical engineering.'

'Yes, I suppose it does, but it's not. I mean that the words are unconfined by the circumstances that would limit and condition and qualify them if they were spoken aloud to someone you knew, in the presence of that person and all the detail of their lives. Letters aren't *interrupted* like that, especially when they are to people you hardly know. They don't have to keep their eye on the listener, the way you have to do in a conversation,' smiling himself, since he was keeping an eye on his listener. 'They don't have to react to all the little gestures of response, the nuances on the listener's face. Writing letters, you can't see the face of the person who is reading them, just as the person who is reading them can't see the face of the person who is writing them. You can't see the reservations and uncertainties and ironies, the tentativeness. You have more freedom to interpret the words the way you want to. They are open-ended, and very vulnerable to desire. It's almost as if the person who receives them can make the sender into the person they *want* to receive them from.'

'So the letters are false then, an illusion.'

'No, not false, I don't mean that at all — maybe in a way they're more the opposite of that, more *true* — but tricky, dangerous.' He would have continued, to say something about how, if interrupted by your interlocutor, a thought you were speaking — that was just developing as you spoke — might never be known, might never grow into the thing that it might have been, but as if to caution him a fine shred of zucchini flower had lodged itself between a molar and his gum, and he tried to work it away with his tongue. It must have seemed as if he had paused for thought.

She looked at him intently — there was a brief, slightly unsettling moment of eye contact, her eyes not as dark as he had thought, but owl-like, grey – and then asked what had made him think so much about letters, as he obviously had, and whether he had experienced something similar, a danger, in correspondence, and, the pause continuing – he didn't quite know what to say, where to begin – began to speculate.

'Claudia was saying something about danger the night before last. We talked for hours after I arrived, on her balcony. Drank too much wine and smoked too many cigarettes and stayed up far too late. And at one point she started to tell me her theory – well, it's not a theory, really – about intimacy, about how dangerous it can be.'

'Intimacy?' The shred of zucchini flower had at last dislodged.

'It wasn't even about intimacy, really, but about tenderness. Perhaps in some ways they are the same thing, or can seem to be. That's the problem. That was her point. That you can act tenderly toward someone, even a stranger, when the circumstances seem to need it or invite it – it's a natural human response, after all, of sympathy, of compassion – and that it can so easily be mistaken for intimacy. People are so thirsty for tenderness, she said, that when they receive even the smallest amount of it, they – well, I was going to say "spill over", but that would be a mixed metaphor, yes? Maybe I should say "rush to drink it all", if I have said "thirsty", but it's actually both these things, a spilling over *and* a rushing to drink, just like that thing, what do you call it?, on the surface of the water in a glass, when it's so full you can see the water is actually above the rim, but there's a kind of skin on it that stops it from spilling.'

An elderly man – seventy-five? eighty? – who had been feeding stale bread to a large flock of pigeons a few metres away in the square finished and shook out a generous spray of crumbs from his worn paper bag – a third of the bag must have been crumbs – then turned and began to walk very slowly away, folding the bag carefully in his trembling hands, his head shaking as if he were tormented by some undislodgeable regret. Parkinson's.

'A meniscus,' Stephen said, having remembered the word.

'Yes, a meniscus. And when you touch it with your finger it breaks, and that extra water, around the rim, spills over. It's as if people are like that.

Not all people, but many. So *full* of this *need*. And when you touch them, even just with a finger, in tenderness, they spill. Do you know what I mean?'

'Yes, indeed. She seems very wise, this friend of yours' – kicking himself immediately for how condescending that must have sounded, not having intended it like that at all, nor to imply that she, Irena, was not wise herself. Indeed she seemed rather disconcertingly wise, or if not – for who was wise, really? – then intelligent, self-aware.

He was going to say that he had often been surprised by how what had been only normal human tenderness on his part had come to seem, had brought about, a kind of awkwardness, because the other person's expectations had suddenly surged, presumed so much more than the touch of the fingers or the softness of voice had actually meant, and he had had to draw lines that he had never envisaged he would have to draw. So that, yes, he had sometimes thought, tenderness was to be handled most carefully, most sparingly, unless one was protected by childhood, or old age, or saintliness. Tenderness was almost a weapon.

But she had come back to the emails.

'And it was like that, *is* like that, with the email.

As if each of us watched for the slightest sign of tenderness, and spilt over when we found it – not suddenly, all at once, but steadily, inevitably. We have been telling each other things that we have not told anyone else. There are things, for example, that he has told me that he has not told his wife, or has not been able to tell her. I don't know about him – I think it is the same for him – but for me it has been as if he understands me, tolerates things about me, accepts things that no one has been able to tolerate or accept before.'

'Perhaps because no one has been told before?' He was trying to avoid any sign of his curiosity about what such intolerable things might be.

'Yes, but that was because I did not feel that they'd . . . because I *knew* that they would not tolerate or accept them.'

'But – well,' shifting his wine glass, since the waiter had arrived with a large salad. Had they ordered salad? but maybe it came with the meal, and it didn't matter, it looked delicious. 'There are two responses here.' Always this tendency to bifurcate. 'Firstly that perhaps you shouldn't be so apprehensive about what people might or might not accept or tolerate. The chances are that whatever you experience, regardless of what others *say*, is probably very human indeed and is experienced over and over and over. And secondly, that perhaps because you do *not* know him . . . or,' seeing that she was about to object to this, 'because you *did* not yet know him, and because, at such distance, in such separate lives, the information was in a sense safe. You were sending it away into a kind of nothingness, emptiness. No "real" relationship depended upon whether or not he would accept it. You could tell him with a kind of impunity.'

'Yes, exactly, yes. And he could tell me similar things.'

'So that in a way you *have* come to know each other quite intimately.'

'Yes, yes, just so. It was a test, though I did not know it, and he has passed the test. And it is starting to hurt, to ache, and I don't know why.'

The pigeons had finished. Every crumb gone. And as if they had all had the same thought at exactly the same time, took off en masse to the other side of the square.

'Maybe,' yet he did not want to appear like this, as if he had answers, 'because you feel exposed and vulnerable, despite all the safety of distance, and need to confirm that you *are* safe, after all. And so you need to see him.'

'Yes, desperately. Otherwise we could go around in circles forever. But this is crazy!'

'Crazy? I don't understand.'

'To be telling you all this, a complete stranger.'

'Because I *am* a complete stranger, and you can tell me with impunity. We just talked about that. I mean, whom could I tell who could possibly affect you? Even if I were inclined to tell, which generally speaking I am not.' ('I am a grave,' one of his teachers had once said. 'Your secret is as safe as if you had buried it.')

'Hah! You see? Crazy!'

'And because, a lot of the time, we don't know what we think until we force it into expression, and we do that mostly through telling someone. If we don't say it, don't get it out that way, then maybe it remains a part of ourselves we don't see, don't know about, a part that doesn't really exist. A total stranger, because they can be told, with impunity, things we can't so easily tell others, might actually help us to come into existence, *particularly*,' and here he was, saying it at last, 'if one is saying it through *letters*.' Vince Sherry telling him that time, at university, so authoritatively, leaning across the bar: *nothing is possessed until it is articulated.* Vince, with his wild hair and huge moustache, his wide eyes. Gone now. So many friends gone now.

'And you are a total stranger, yes?'

'Yes,' he said. 'A total stranger, as you are to me.'

'A field of potential.'

'Yes.' He smiled. 'I suppose so. A field of potential.'

PRIMO PIATTO

———— ◈◈◈◈◈◈◈◈◈◈◈◈ ————

The waiter came with their next course, warning them that the dishes were very hot, hovering
with them while he and Irena moved their wine
glasses clear. Two wide-rimmed, steaming bowls,
his of a larger-than-expected portion of pasta,
hers, as she soon explained, of handmade potato
and spinach gnocchi with garlic, basil, tiny
tomatoes, the best oil, the best olives. The conversation broke as they settled again, arranged
themselves, scented, tasted. He was surprisingly
hungry, as if the night, the air, the conversation had whetted his appetite, and at the same
time had drifted them momentarily into calmer
waters, within their own separate thoughts. The
waiter returned with a small grater of some kind

and a large wooden peppermill tucked under his arm. He held the grater over Stephen's bowl and glanced at him for a signal.

'*Tartufo*,' Irena said, 'just as a garnish. There is probably already plenty in the dish.' And so he tried an enthusiastic '*Sì! Sì!*' and the waiter grated a generous sprinkling over the centre of the steaming pile of noodles, then turned gallantly to her, asking, in Italian, whether she would like some also. She nodded enthusiastically, watching wide-eyed as the flakes fell. He gestured next with the peppermill and, when each of them nodded, twisted it liberally over her gnocchi, a little less so over the priests.

A minute went by. It may have been longer. They were savouring the moment, but as it continued he felt an old anxiety hovering, that feeling that the silence was somehow his responsibility, that it meant that someone – he – was failing . . . and then felt it strangely receding, heard her saying, without her saying it, something about the absurdity of such a feeling, that the silence was after all a natural thing, something that did not need filling. Savour. There is no pressure. Nothing to be filled. The silence is a fullness in itself.

'Well,' he said, after what can't have been more than a minute, 'this looks wonderful! And enough for two of me. I'm glad I didn't order *secondi*!'

'*Secondo*. Yes,' she replied, 'the servings are very generous. I didn't order a main course either. I am hungry and the gnocchi are one of my favourite things, but they are also heavy. You can feel full after surprisingly little. I have learnt to eat them slowly,' – she smiled – 'to give my stomach time to expand.'

The clouds that had come in soon after the unexpected gust and had stayed for the next hour had now cleared, as if a higher and gentler breeze had picked up, a long way above them. The very last of the sunset, breaking through, cast long shadows, gave whatever it fell upon a rich, almost painterly glow. He thought to comment upon the strange warmth of the evening, to say that he had anticipated that he would have to move inside at some point, but felt no need to. The tea-candles in their shining cubes were turning each table into its own small island. And his glass was empty. He had been waiting for her to finish hers. When she did so he asked whether he should order some more. They had just started their main course and she had been right, the *teran* would accompany it so well. The waiter, when he caught his eye, seemed to have anticipated his gesture, nodded, and moved off toward the inner door. Before he went inside, he seated, with the greatest courtesy, an elderly couple at the table with the *Riservato* sign. In their late seventies perhaps, or older, tall, dignified, immaculately dressed. She with a walking-stick. Pearls around her slender neck. An aura about them. They might have been movie stars. From a Fellini film. *Amarcord*.

And then, as so often happens, he and Irena both began speaking at once. He caught himself, stopped. Each of them insisted the other continue. She was embarrassed, she said. What she had been going to say was a frivolous thing.

'Frivolous? Now I am intrigued.'

'No, no. You were about to say something. Please. I have taken enough time, with my dilemma. Please.'

'It's just that, well, your story of how your grandfather and grandmother came together – you know, his hitch-hiking into the mountains to find her after the war – reminded me of my own father and mother.'

'Reminded you? Really? Is their story similar?'

'Yes. At least in that they are both of wartime meetings, and post-war returns. And I imagine they would be about the same age, my parents and your grandparents, if they were alive. Is your grandmother alive?'

'No. She died when I was five.'

'And neither are my parents. My father died ten years ago and my mother almost twenty years before that. My father was from the New Hebrides too. I don't know if you know about the New Hebrides. They are called Vanuatu now. But for a long time, as the New Hebrides, they were under what was described as a condominium government, French and English at the same time. My father's parents, my own grandfather and grandmother, were from the British side. My grandfather had been a minor official, but when his wife died – when my father was only ten – he went a little crazy. With grief, I suppose, or perhaps it was just what they call going *troppo*.'

'*Troppo*!' She smiled. '"Too much"! I like that.'

'Yes, but in this case it means succumbing to the tropics, becoming a little wild, ragged, letting oneself go. He bought a small coconut plantation and moved out to it, but showed far more interest in drinking than in growing coconuts. My father stayed with friends in the capital – not as large a town as that sounds, but at least he could continue to go to school – and I guess he and his father became pretty estranged. Eventually his father took up with a native woman from a French part of the island. She'd had a daughter by a Frenchman, a trader, who had literally sailed off and left her. When she went to live with my grandfather this girl, her daughter, must have been fifteen or sixteen. By that stage the war had started, and my father had just finished school. He went back to live with my grandfather to find this woman and her daughter in residence. Things weren't very pleasant, apparently, but I guess my father and the daughter, my mother, got along . . .'

'Your mother?'

'Yes. My father stayed around for almost a year, but eventually had a final falling out with his father, and left for Australia, to enlist. Britain was too hard to get to by this time, and Singapore had just fallen, and I guess he felt the most useful thing he could do would be to fight for the Australians. He went to New Caledonia first, and then somehow found his way to Brisbane, and eventually became a war hero, fighting in New Guinea. After the war, in Australia, he took advantage of a government scheme to go to university. And that's where the stories become similar. He had just finished his second year examinations – this is the old family story – and an army friend who had a yacht asked him to go ocean sailing. My father loved sailing. He said it was the only thing that kept him sane that year he'd tried to live with his own father – that, and my mother. And it stirred something up in him, this one day on the ocean with his friend. He said that the night afterward, or the night after that, he had sat bolt upright in bed with the sudden realisation that he was in love with my mother, the daughter of his father's lover, and had to get to her as soon as possible. It was the beginning of December. He went straight to his army friend – the one with the yacht – and within a week they were sailing back toward the New Hebrides.'

'Sailing? How far is that?'

'About three thousand kilometres from Sydney, but even longer the way they did it, since they sailed up the east coast, to get used to things, before sailing out across the Pacific. I guess, you know, after the intensity of the war experience, civilian life left them feeling a bit beached. They were probably both longing for adventure. And the danger of it would probably have seemed nothing compared with the war they had just been through.'

'Still, it is incredible! And this girl, your mother, did she know he was coming?'

'No. He calculated – wrongly, I suspect – that a letter would take longer to get there than it would take them to sail. And they had never exchanged any letters anyway. He didn't even know if she was still there.'

'But she was.'

'Yes, she was. A nurse, in Santo, the main French town. They went straight to see his father – moored just off the coconut plantation – to find out where she was. The native woman, her mother, was gone, and his father, far from being overjoyed to see him, was furious about the whole thing. But her location slipped out anyway and they went to her. She used to say that she had never been all that surprised, that she had known that he would come. Just not in a yacht, that way. And within a week they were married. A wedding in her mother's village. His father – my grandfather – didn't come.'

'And they sailed back?'

'Yes. They sailed back. And my father finished university and became a public servant, in the Department of Foreign Affairs, and they had three children, my brother, my sister and me. We lived in Canberra for a while but then he got a top job in the New South Wales government and we moved to Sydney, where we could live beside the ocean. Both my father and my mother loved the ocean. My mother would swim every day, the whole length of the beach, and it was a long beach. Right up until her death.'

'A swimmer! I am a swimmer too! I would love to live on a beach! And such a romantic story.'

'Yes. Almost as romantic as partisan love. But you were going to ask something, before you got me started on that.'

'Oh, just about that kiss, you know? I was going to ask if you had ever had such a kiss. Something, how do you say it? that stole your breath, that shocked you like that, that left you shaking?'

'I suppose every relationship starts like that, or most of them, with *something* like that. If the first kiss or kisses aren't very appealing then it's hard to see why one would continue. I've always thought they indicated something about a person's personality.' Remembering Carol's kisses, which had been always slightly awkward, slightly tight-mouthed, with that sharp, darting tongue, no real relaxation, no real welcome or openness, and yet that had been eight years, and two children. 'But in fact there was a kiss that I was remembering, as you talked about yours.' One he had often thought about. Part of the mind's cache.

'So, tell me.'

'It was while I was in Canada on that high school exchange. I was there from September, when school started, until February. It was exciting for me. I'd never experienced a winter like that. So much snow! There is *never* snow in Sydney.

'I had made some Jewish friends, and at Christmas, when the universities had a short break, one of their friends, I think a cousin, came back from her university to see her family for a few days. She was exotic to me. Older than us by a year or two, and so beautiful that I couldn't take my eyes off her. Long black hair, full lips, beautiful eyes, and a kind of atmosphere around her that was, I don't know, *seraphic*. And to my great surprise she started talking with me straightaway, and we got along well, almost instantly. She was very interested in Australia, and asking questions about the deserts and the animals and so forth, and on my side I was talking about how strange and wonderful the snow was to me. She had a car, a red Mustang, probably her parents' car, and arranged the next day to pick me up and take me for a drive in the countryside. I thought she was just saying it to be polite, but she turned up exactly on time and we drove out through fields covered in snow, and into the forest. She stopped and we took a walk. I should say that she was a smoker – smoked menthol cigarettes – and she smoked one as we walked. At some point a hundred metres or so from the car, she leant back against a tree and we kissed, and it was, yes, one of those kisses. Open and warm and soft, no hardness or confusion, with the winter chill on her lips and her cheeks, and the hint of smoke, the touch of menthol, and there was a scent about her – I don't know – some other scent, that I have never found again. And yes, it left me trembling. And I have remembered it all this time. As if it were somehow definitive. And I don't know her name any more, can't remember it: I think it was

Laurel, or Laura, but I'm not sure. It was so long ago. I'm sure I thought then that I would never forget it, but it seems I have.'

'But not the kiss.'

'No, not the kiss.'

'Laura. A famous name, among lovers. Let it be Laura then. Perfect for her. The smoke, the scent, the winter chill, snow. *L'aura*. Petrarca. But of course he never even touched his Laura. A married woman. Did you know she was the wife of an ancestor of the Marquis de Sade? But you were luckier. You got to kiss her. What happened then?'

'Nothing. She took me home with that kiss still hanging between us, and drove off – she was late for something – and I never saw her again.'

'Perfect. Just the way it should have been.'

The waiter arrived with what appeared to be the remains of the bottle of *teran* from which their first glasses had been poured, and asked how they had liked it, explained where it had come from, only ten or twelve kilometres away, directly north, over the Slovenian border. He filled their glasses, placed the bottle between them – it almost seemed as if he were making a gift of it – and moved on to another table.

'What *is* love, do you think? I mean, no, not quite that, but how do you *know* when you are in love? I mean . . . Ah, no, sorry, it's too huge!'

He couldn't help the briefest of chuckles, stifled as soon as he saw the flash of confused anger in her eye.

'No, no!' he said immediately, trying to head off the affront. 'I wasn't laughing at your question! Far from it! It's just that, well, you're asking me, an Australian male, and some would say we are the least likely to be of any help with such an issue. We are supposed to be so emotionally reserved, so ham-fisted!'

'But I'm not asking "an Australian male",' she said, calming. 'I'm asking you. And besides, why would an Australian male be any less likely than a Russian, or an Italian, for that matter?'

'I don't know. Maybe you're right.' He wanted to answer, after all, or at least to try, since the question had troubled him often enough in the past. 'I used to think it was a verbal thing, or at least partly verbal.'

'A verbal thing? How could it be a verbal thing? It's a matter of the heart, surely.'

'I don't mean that it's exclusively verbal. But it's as if the word "love" itself is a kind of barrier, or border to be crossed. You find yourself in the territory – and it seems fairly clear, when you're in that kind of territory – but it's up to you, something in you, whether you cross that border or you don't.'

'Cross it? I don't understand.'

'Whether you say "I love you" or not. I know it sounds tautological, but I've sometimes thought that one of the principal indications as to whether you love someone or not is whether you decide to take that leap, and *say* it.'

'Some people say it too easily.'

'Yes, maybe, and some people can never say it, almost choke on it.'

'I wonder if that means that they *don't* love, or just that they can't *say* it.'

'I'm sure you can love without saying it. I'm sure there are millions of people who love, but hardly ever say it, or who never say it, but realise at some point during it or after that they are or were in love.'

She looked at him quizzically, as if something he had been saying had not quite added up – had he contradicted himself? – then turned her attention back to her meal. He took a sip of wine, swilled it thoughtfully, calmed. It seemed only now that the full pungency of his own meal revealed itself, after the first physical heat of the dish had receded. Musky, intense. He picked out a flake of what he presumed must be the truffle itself – not one of the gratings the waiter had added – and, though he searched for it, could get no real flavour, yet every other flavour in the dish – mushrooms, garlic, cheese (or was it cream?), oil, the pasta itself – seemed intensified, invested with the truffle's muskiness.

'It's the oil.' She seemed to be reading his mind. 'They put in some shavings of the *tartufo* as they cook, and then some on top afterward, but mainly the flavour is in the oil. Good olive oil that they have drowned – is that how you say it, "drowned"? –'

'"Steeped"?'

'Yes, perhaps, "steeped" pieces of *tartufo* in. The more pieces and the more finely cut, the more intense the flavour of the oil becomes, and the more intensely it flavours the pasta.'

'Well, this is pretty intense. Wonderful in fact. They must have put a lot of truffle in the oil.'

'So,' she said, returning to the previous subject, 'it is *not* a verbal thing?'

'No, as I said, it's not verbal exclusively, but the verbal is still part of it, a big part. A step. A sign. You hold yourself back, *don't* say it, and so many things don't happen. You open yourself out, like you have, in your letters with the Russian.'

'*Lay* yourself out.'

'Lay yourself out, yes, and *say* it. Surely there was a moment in an email – you *told* me there was! – when you paused, and then decided to go ahead and use the word "love"? and things could suddenly happen that might never have happened otherwise.'

'But the word has to stand for something that has already happened, that is already there, yes? – otherwise you wouldn't need to find the word for it in the first place. You make it sound, somehow, as if it is the word that *makes* it happen, brings it into being. As if there's a choice about it. For me there's no choice.'

'You might not be able to say that *saying* it *made* it happen, but it was certainly a catalyst. The appearance of the word, you could say, is a moment of entry . . .'

'Yes, but entry into what?'

'There is no objective test. There is no set of questions that you can answer and if, say, you get seven out of ten then you are clearly and indisputably in love. There isn't a blood-test you can do, or a machine that you can hook yourself up to. People will enter, will start to use the word, at different levels, different stages, for any number of different reasons. It's a position as much as a thing, a place . . .'

'That's a – how do you call it? – a cop-out, not an answer at all.' She seemed dismayed, as if he should have a better response. He felt pushed. Perhaps, if he dug deeper, there would be a better answer. Perhaps there were answers behind answers.

'Then what do *you* think? How would you define it?'

'I don't know. That's why I asked. To me it just arrives, suddenly, a realisation. Pfoof!! To me it feels like being punched in the breast' – and her hands moved suddenly there, and her voice seemed haltered, her eyes wide with an almost frightened wonder, a meniscus, and he remembered it, the Wheel, that might at last be releasing him but was probably just catching her up, for that long journey, so that everything that she now said had a doubleness, a shadow – 'and the word is just there, is just obvious. As if it was the word for the punch as much as for the emotion. But maybe that is just infatuation, or a sudden flood of desire. Maybe, if I thought about it more, I'd say that love itself was something that came after, when you begin to come a little more back to your senses, but only a little. A longing, a feeling that someone has stepped out of a whole crowd of people that you have been moving through in your life, and this person is different, and there is a deep connection. There is no choice about it.'

'But isn't it possible that those people, people whom you might fall in love with, are around all the time, and that you just don't see any one of them in that light until you're ready to, and that it's *other* things that make you ready to? I mean, what do you say to the possibility that you could change crowds, move to a different city, a different country, and there would still be someone, at the point when you were ready, stepping out of the crowd?'

'No, it's more than that. There may be more than one person you could fall in love with, but it is still a matter of that connection, as if you've known them before, maybe, or they *matched* you.'

'Recognised you?'

'Yes, *recognised*, yes! That is good! As if there might have been all these people in your life before, but no one has quite seen who you were, has *recognised* who you were.'

'Yes, but they . . . forgive me, but they could be ugly as sin and misery, as my mother used to say, or twice your age, or in some other way utterly unappealing, and still *recognise* you.'

'Why would twice my age matter? Or ugliness? Have you ever seen a *tartufo*? They are, how did you say it? "ugly as sin and misery". Yet they are hundreds of euros for a kilogram, and many, many people desire them, just like you, tonight. But of course there's more, something else.'

'Yes, they have to fit a kind of profile: they have to be of a certain age, maybe, and a certain physical attractiveness.'

'I have met several men who have been *attractive* to me, and have been close to some of them, slept with them, have had relationships with them, and one or two of them,' here she smiled, broadly, 'have been quite ugly indeed.'

'But the word hasn't happened?'

'Sometimes it has, yes.'

'And do you think that it was love?'

'Well, I have thought so, obviously, at those times. And then, sometimes, later, thought that it wasn't, *realised* that it wasn't, that I had been mistaken, that the recognition stopped somewhere. That at some point there was some part of me that wasn't recognised, or wasn't recognising. Usually it was that something had emerged, become apparent, to myself, that needed to be known and understood by the other person, but wasn't. And . . .'

'And?'

'And, I don't know. Sometimes I haven't quite been able to work out what that thing was, even for myself. Just a feeling of dissatisfaction. As if a battery had run down. There was a passion there but it went, or maybe I thought it was passion but it turned out to be need, infatuation, lust, an experiment.'

'Those are pretty important things!'

'Yes, but you want them to last.'

'Can they?'

'What do you mean? I mean, how do *you* feel? Have you been in relationships where they have gone – faded – or haven't been there in the first place? Would *you* be content with that kind of relationship? *Have* you been content? . . . I don't know. I'm sorry. I shouldn't ask these things. How are your priests?' He had been eating steadily away.

'All dead, I think. One or two of them struggled.' Her unexpected laughter was warm, low, melodic. 'But I think they're all dead.' He was surprised to realise that he had almost finished his bowl. 'And I've enjoyed them immensely . . .'

As if almost unconsciously – certainly he saw no sign of self-consciousness – she reached out with her fork and took, for herself, the very last of his *strozzapreti*: a gesture of some intimacy and yet made so naturally, so apparently unpremeditatedly that he might not have noticed it, though later he would remember, in detail, the feeling at the back of his scalp – it was as if someone had just touched him – and the brief trickle of the sauce, from the corner of her mouth, caught back by and then licked from the crook of her finger.

'And of course,' he said, hoping it would appear to be almost without pause, 'you should ask those things. We are perfect strangers, remember? And if we can't take advantage, to ask these things . . .'

'Well?'

'Well, for a start I would say that that might be a kind of ideal, a wonderful thing to happen when it can, but it doesn't always happen, and maybe it *can't* always happen. A lot of people, most people maybe, aren't fortunate enough to experience it. I mean, look around you, at these people passing by right now,' and he gestured perhaps too readily, without really looking, to the cluster of people at one end of the fountain at the centre of the piazza – an overweight couple in their thirties or forties, a buck-toothed, large-nosed young woman in bright pink slacks, an older man in a trench-coat carrying a worn leather briefcase under his arm, a beggar-woman with a sun-worn face that looked like a piece of gnarled wood, a council worker in a green jacket, leaning against a broom, smoking, at the end of his day.

'That's prejudice! That's almost disgusting. It's elitist!' It was half amusement, but also half genuine alarm.

'Yes, of course it is,' embarrassed yet again, 'and I don't mean to be, I'm sorry, but isn't it also true? Not about these people particularly, but do you really think that everyone experiences a grand passion? that nobody compromises? that people don't *make* love, *construct* it, when they can't *find* it? that they don't put it together, out of available materials? Maybe it's the grand passion kind of discussion that is elitist. Most people probably just settle for what they can get. Arrangements, companionship, someone to be with them, help them with their business, raise a family with.'

'And recognise them.'

'Yes, okay, and recognise them, yes. And be with them in their illnesses, and as they are dying. But passion doesn't have to be a part of that. And at some point the word *love* will probably have come to them, and they will have decided to use it, they will have worked their way into it.'

She looked sceptical again. Her eyes cast about

for a moment, then, as if some other thought had struck her, seemed to lead her to turn her head left-ward, toward the sea, which had darkened entirely, was now a black expanse dotted with lights. Ships in the bay. Ships at night. And silence, once more, in which they were both thinking. In the background he saw the waiter bring a course to the elegant elderly couple on the table that had had the *Riservato* sign. So far he hadn't seen them utter a word. And yet they seemed peaceful enough, content. Perhaps they didn't need words.

'Anyway,' she said, turning back toward him, 'I don't think you have answered me.'

'Answered you?'

'Yes, about *your* experience. Has it ever happened to you? Have you ever been in a relationship when the passion, the recognition, have gone, or when they perhaps weren't really there in the first place? But of course you have; your wife, the divorce.'

'Yes. True. Perhaps a better question would be have I ever been in a relationship when it *hasn't* gone.'

'And how have you dealt with it, when it's gone?'

'Not always well . . . But now, you see, the question is becoming very large indeed, or the answer is.' And here it was his turn to look, past her, toward the dark bay. It was not really that he was overwhelmed – he would have liked to explain to her – but that he feared he might well be, if he progressed much further. A horn sounded, from somewhere far out, long and deep. One of the great tankers, perhaps, that he'd seen earlier, out on the horizon. Moving.

INSALATA

She shifted her attention to the salad, began to eat
it from the large central bowl, rather than serv-
ing it out to her side plate. A domestic habit, it
seemed to him, intimate but also childlike. Had
she been his daughter, in a restaurant such as this,
he might once have told her to be more polite. But
then he smiled at himself. She ate with a relish and
unselfconsciousness that was a pleasure to watch.
She looked up, her mouth full, and they made eye-
to-eye contact, held it a second longer than they
might, and she smiled broadly, gesturing him with
her fork to join her. He did so, and by her method.
It was delicious. Small lamb's-tongue lettuce,
mache, with tomato, some of the same large green
olives he had been brought before, tiny leaves of

rocket, capers, a perfect dressing, every flavour distinct. Including one that, although strangely familiar, he couldn't identify.

'This is good,' he said, and then asked about the taste, some herb? There were small pieces of something white, that he had thought might be garlic but then, bitten into, had told him nothing.

'The wild fennel? There's just a little of it – a bit of the stalk, perhaps? the rest of the plant is too, how do you say it? like wire, or plastic – though it might also be the capers.'

'No,' he said, 'not the capers. It must be the fennel.' Now he recognised the touch of aniseed, a taste that normally did not appeal to him but this was different, in the subtlety, the mere hint of it. The bowl was now almost empty. Reaching for one of the last few capers, he remembered an eccentric aunt's emphatic, know-it-all declaration one Christmas dinner in his late teens, that capers came from a particular Mediterranean seaweed. And he had believed it for years, although perhaps he should have known. The same aunt, Betty – she wasn't an aunt really, but a distant English cousin of his father's who'd come to ground in Sydney, not far from them – with her long white hair and thick black walking-stick, had once dressed a salad with leaves from a herb they couldn't recognise. Bitter, horrible. When they had asked about the flavour she'd insisted it was basil, and eventually showed them the plant. A weed, lovingly tendered, in a large, cracked terracotta pot, a sticky weed. The basil, if it had ever been there, had died long ago, but its rival was luxurious.

'Have you ever seen a caper bush?' she asked, and when he told her that he'd only ever seen photographs, recounted her own story, of the first time she had seen them, only four years before. Presumably they had been around her all her life, but she had never noticed them. She had just begun to share the apartment with Claudia. Claudia was part Slovenian. Her father, who had died some ten years earlier, had been from Pirano. Claudia's mother had never been comfortable with her husband's relatives, but had been invited to lunch, after a long period of silence, and she felt that she should go, but she wanted moral support.

'Claudia and I had already made plans. We were going to visit Venice for the day. But her mother pleaded with us, and insisted that I come too. The relatives couldn't be so bad, really, and Pirano was charming, beautiful. We could see Pirano that weekend, and go to Venice the next.

'And it is true. Pirano is very nice. Not exactly a miniature Venice, though it seems once to have thought of itself that way. A piazza right on the water and here and there in the stonework around it the same, you know, *winged lion* from the top of the plinth in the Piazza San Marco.

'But driving in the town is almost impossible. We had to park in the piazza and then walk up a long stony street – what is the word, "cobbled"? – toward the top of the town. They call it the street of the suicides, or at least Claudia's father's family did, because it leads up to a point on a cliff where many people jump. And all along the street were these caper bushes growing out of the stone walls. Claudia's mother told us that her husband had been convinced in his childhood that the saltiness of the capers came from the tears of the broken-hearted young men and women as they walked up the street, in the night, to throw themselves from the cliff. But of course it comes only from the pickling. They are flower-buds, capers – tiny flower-buds.'

'There's a place in Sydney where they do that – throw themselves from a cliff. It's called The Gap.

It looks out onto the Pacific. No caper bushes there. A rock shelf, way below, that the waves wash over.' Sad, windy place, overcast any time he'd visited. Suicides, murders. And a lighthouse, somewhere around there. What was it called? Barrenjoey? No. Macquarie. The Macquarie Light.

'Really? Well, I suppose all cities have to have their suicide places, though probably not all of them are so picturesque. In Pirano it's also a matter of legend. On the way up to the house, almost at the top of the hill – Claudia's relatives were the second or third house from the cliff's edge – there is a church with a very tall campanile. I had seen it from the piazza where we parked. It dominates the town. It looked as if it would have an impressive view. On our way back, I got Claudia to come into the church with me to see if we could get up somehow. There was an old man there, a sort of caretaker, who spoke Italian and who was happy to unlock the gate and take us up, and when we got to the top – it really was very high, with a broad panorama of the sea – he told us the story of the Beautiful Vida. He said it was a kind of folk tale, several hundred years old. Vida was supposedly the most beautiful woman in all the surrounding country, and she had fallen in love with this Moor who had seduced her and then sailed away, abandoning her. Apparently she would go up to the top of this very tower day after day for years to look out over the sea, watching for his return, but then at some point she must have had a premonition of some kind, or just finally given up, and she had leapt from the tower to her death on the stones below.'

'A Moor, who abandoned her! It sounds like *Othello*.'

'Yes, well, that was set in Venice, wasn't it? And so the region is right – Pirano as the little Venice. And the Vida story is old enough. But it gets better. There are other versions. I liked the story and I got curious, mainly because the old man's version had had so few details. It turns out that it's a kind of Slovenian national legend, although the versions I found – I could only find two or three – were quite different from his. According to those, Vida was the wife of an older man and had had a sickly child, a son, by him. She was very unhappy in her marriage and would come down to the sea shore, supposedly to wash clothes, but in fact to weep. One day a Moorish sailor found her there and, when he heard her story, told her to come with him – he worked for the Queen of Spain – and she would have a much happier life. On impulse, and perhaps because she was so attracted to this sailor, she sailed with him to Spain, and became a handmaiden to the Queen. But she regretted what she had done and began to long for her child and her earlier life. Supposedly she would go to a tower in the castle every day – the versions start to seem like mirror images of one another – and look out to sea, toward where she thought her home would be, and weep. According to one version there was an old cherry tree below the window of the tower – a barren tree, nearly dead – and her tears, over the seven years that she did this, revived it and it began to flower again.'

'The capers! And the tears of the suicides!'

'Yes. It's a kind of mirror story in that way too.'

'Is that it?' He felt left high and dry. 'Did she ever make it home?'

'According to one story, yes. The sailor, who had become her lover, eventually felt pity for her in her sadness and took her home. She met three young boys on the beach when she got there, and one of them was her son. But according to another version she jumped from the tower.'

'Like the old man said she did.'

'Yes. Like the old man said.'

They finished the salad. He was half-hoping for another caper, to taste the saltiness again, but they had gone, leaving, he imagined, the trace of themselves in the small pool of dressing at the bottom of the bowl. Had he been alone he might have dipped the last of his bread into it.

'Have you ever thought about suicide?' The question unsettled him a little. There seemed nothing she wouldn't ask about.

'No,' he replied, 'not really. I mean, I have, thought about it, but only that, thought about it, envisioned it, asked myself whether I was the kind of person who might do it, whether it might be an option. But the answer has always been negative. Have you?'

'Once,' she said, but offered nothing more, despite the hovering silence. Had she taken a wrong turning? Her eyes, for a moment, moved to the ground beside him, as if watching some dark thing scamper from the table, but then flicked up again, almost defensively. He might have seen something he should not have. At the end of a long, dark corridor. A door closing.

'I don't know what I would do, without passion, or the anticipation of it,' she resumed, after a long pause. 'I seem to be able to manage without it for long pieces of time, but when it comes, I don't know. It seems to eat me almost, obsess me. I sometimes think I must be what they call a dangerous woman.'

'Dangerous? How?' He thought of complimenting her, saying how unlikely it was that someone so beautiful and so sensible could be dangerous, but realised that that was an old impulse in him, obvious and empty and rote, and that they were in any case already well past that. And in a way he suspected that he knew what she meant. And could remember being racked. The Wheel. But should ask nonetheless.

'That there is something about me that will hurt others.'

'Do you *want* to hurt others?' It seemed unlikely, and that she was exaggerating somehow, although the what of it was not clear.

'No, of course not, but unintentionally, as a by-product, of desire.'

'Is yours ever the only desire involved?'

'No, but I could be more cautious, have better judgement.'

'Is desire a matter of judgement?'

'No, maybe not, but it could be. Maybe we could try to make it so; maybe love is.'

'Maybe it is, but maybe judgement is more complicated than we know.'

'How do you mean?'

'Surely the past is part of the judgement, the kinds of desires it sets up in us. And the body; the body is part of it too.' And magic, and spells, and weather, the wind. Who on earth knew?

'The body? What do you mean?'

'Surely the body has its own needs and times, finds itself ready for something, demands it. The push of biology in us. And we have got to the point in this civilisation where the shapes of our lives, the other things we are doing, the other drives we are following, are very often out of step with the body's rhythms, and we're twisted and crippled, messed up, by our consciousness as the mind tries to grapple with something that isn't really a matter of mind in the first place.

'I had a friend once who used to argue that everything was biological, that our only purpose on earth was to reproduce and raise our offspring, and that everything else, all of culture, everything we associate with civilisation – music, literature, philosophy – was just distraction, something to divert us.' How much of our lives spent sleeping, shitting, pissing, thinking about sex, eating, preparing to eat, cleaning up after eating. What was the culture-space, the working-space? five or six hours a day? The rest all a matter of the body: maintaining it, fuelling it, getting it from one place to another.

'As for being a "dangerous" woman, a "dangerous" man,' trying to focus himself again, 'if we're talking about love, certainly I think I have hurt others, because of it. But if we think of the danger to ourselves, which we should probably also do, how do you calculate that? Isn't it likely to be in proportion to the extent of our feelings? And so there is, isn't there, some balance to it? Couldn't you almost say that someone is "dangerous" to *us* to the extent that we *love* them? But isn't the danger in some sort of proportion to the reward? And can one have that kind of reward, the intense pleasure that love can be, without the risk, the danger?

'It's always seemed a great paradox to me, a kind of absurdity I can never really get my mind around, that love can be such an amazing pleasure, such an astonishing thing, such a gift, an ecstasy at times, and yet we seem in a way to resent it so much and can be so broken, so devastated, when it goes. As if it were a drug, an addiction, and we have to undergo withdrawal. We become *so sad about having been so happy*, when surely another option is being glad, being grateful for the gift of it in the first place, thankful for what we had. Preserving the joy of it, cutting the Gordian knot between joy and sorrow.'

'The Gordian knot?' She seemed pleased at the term. 'Yes, I suppose it is. I hadn't thought of it like that. I wonder what makes it so tight in the first place, that knot, between joy and sorrow.'

'Human selfishness probably, a kind of narcissism that assesses everything by its effect upon ourselves. And a desire to possess. Not much different from what makes us want better and better houses, better and better cars.'

'I don't know about the houses and the cars. That's all too cynical. And besides, without the desire for better and better cars I'd be without a job! But Narcissus looked into a pool, yes? and was in love with his own image. Maybe love *is* a little like that. While we are in love we are looking into the lover as if into a pool and seeing ourselves, and being "in love" is a kind of being *held together* by the other person. We love them because they somehow reflect us, and when they go, when we lose them, we are shattered, we don't feel that we hold together any more.'

'Another part of that business of recognition. Who knows? But that's my point. Surely there is a kind of love that can be less narcissistic because it comes from a stronger sense of self, a love that doesn't risk dissolution like that, or that pendulum-swing into mourning.'

'Maybe.' She paused, thinking. 'Maybe there is this one thing which we have been calling love, and there are just different human reactions to it, or maybe there *are* different kinds of love. And hence the confusion. All of us talking about it as if it were the one thing when in fact there are many and it is not all that often that we are actually talking about the same thing. The person who says "I love you" and the person to whom it is said might have different understandings of it entirely. So our confusions, at least some of them, could be, what do you call them? errors of classification?'

'Well, that is quite a conversation stopper,' he said after a few seconds, watching her eyes search somewhere above and behind him, as if trying to hold sight of a thought. Indeed she seemed to have stopped herself. 'But you may be right. When we were talking just now about how it was that sorrow seems so tied to love sometimes . . .'

'The Gordian knot, yes . . .' There was a tiredness in her. Had he been pushing too hard, thinking it was a conversation only, when maybe there were other things involved, unstated, unstatable?

'Well, you know,' he would try to continue more carefully, 'I was thinking that in some cases it's even stronger than that, that there are some people for whom it's not just a kind of *tristesse*, you know, a sorrow that comes when love ends or doesn't work out, but for whom love is always and almost inextricably associated with pain, even as it happens, as if pain – drama, tragedy – is almost a constant of love.'

'*Tristesse.* The sadness you are supposed to feel, after making love. They say it comes especially after you make love with someone you don't know.'

'Really? I hadn't heard that, but I suppose it makes sense.' Trying to remember who there had been who had experienced it. Carol? Who would sometimes lie there, afterward, weeping quietly into her pillow. As if he had been cruel somehow, had hurt her without knowing it, no matter how tender he had tried to be. Had she ever known him? Was that it? Had he kept himself unknown? But there had always been something else there, out of reach, a negative as deeply entrenched as his supposedly infuriating positive. Negative. *The* Negative. Sometimes he had felt that it was that that he was fighting, not her.

'Maybe,' he would chance it, 'it comes down to something else, a kind of love of *being*, or the lack of it, because without that I can't really see how any of the other kinds of love are going to work so well.'

'How do you mean?'

'How can you really love someone else if you don't love being alive, if you aren't excited by existence itself? If you aren't excited by existence like that, *in love with being*, then it seems to me that any other kind of love is going to be handicapped from the start, skewed, twisted, even more selfish. You're going to be asking it to compensate for the world somehow, putting extra pressure on it. In a way it's going to be a love that's built upon a kind of repulsion.'

'But the world can be a very horrible place. It's not hard to see how people might find it difficult to love.'

'Yes, of course. I'm not saying that it isn't a horrid place, in a lot of ways, but it is also the *only* place, and even that perception of horror can be based – usually is – on a sort of love of being. Otherwise where would the feeling of horror, the revulsion come from?

'Sorry,' remembering Carol, her negativity that could leave love so stranded, 'that's getting a bit philosophical, I guess, another conversation stopper . . .' There had been, in the past, so many other long conversations about love, but they had been so painful, so anguished. ('How *could* you?', 'I can't *believe* that you . . .': love as a tether, a rein; love dipped in madness, mutual despair, barely recognisable for what it once was.)

'No. It's not a conversation stopper at all!' Again it was as if she was reading his thoughts. 'It seems to me that you're talking about something fundamental. It might stop *your* conversation for a moment but it won't stop mine!' – smiling, leading him carefully away from the pit. 'I still have many questions. I am young. You are ancient. I am presuming that you have been to many places and done many things. You are tied to the chair by my charm and the wonder of the night, or perhaps just by arthritis or too much *teran*, and I have questions.'

Now she was teasing him outright. And closer to the truth than bore dwelling on.

'It is not too much *teran*,' he said, smiling too. 'I don't know about the other things. Though the night, yes, is wonderful,' and would have said, Yes, the spell she was casting, but again thought better of it. 'So?'

'So?'

'Questions. You have questions. Ask me. I am at your disposal.' Suddenly – was it the spell? – he was needing to tell, whatever she wanted.

'Has it ever happened to you, that you have found a way to cut the knot? Had a relationship where sorrow didn't follow the joy?'

'Not often. On my side – from my own per-spective, my own feelings – it comes and goes. In some relationships that I have had, I have not seemed to be dependent in that way, haven't really felt at risk, so much so that sometimes I've actually wondered – how is this for throwing the conver-sation sideways? – whether perhaps I didn't really know how to love in the first place, whether I was somehow incapable of loving properly.'

'If you worry about it then you're probably quite capable of loving properly. But that's not an answer. I was asking about the knot, between joy and sorrow. Have you ever cut it?'

'Sometimes. Once. Once I think I glimpsed something, a different kind of possibility.'

'A different kind of possibility?'

'It's not a very noble story on my part, but on hers it's not so bad. It was while I was in university. My second summer. I had worked for a while as a labourer and saved enough for a hitch-hiking holiday in North America. Well, not hitch-hiking really, it was far too cold, the middle of winter, so mainly it was buses. Greyhound buses. A long story. I was doing a kind of pilgrimage to some of the places that the Beat poets wrote about – you know, Jack Kerouac? Gary Snyder? – and I began in San Francisco, visiting a friend of a friend. I'd just been given his address, nothing more, but he was very kind, showed me around. He was at college there and while I was staying his girlfriend was there also, from Los Angeles, where she was studying. We all became close, in a very short period of time, it was a memorable visit, and before she left she invited me to come to see her, if I managed to make it to Los Angeles.

'I went north and then east on my pilgrimage but on my way back, before flying out, I went to Los Angeles, specially to see her. It was a weekend. She showed me around on the first day – she had a car – but there was nowhere for me to sleep except in her college room.

'It was easy, natural. We went to bed together as if there had never been any question about it, and made love for two nights and a day. Ferocious, passionate, exhausting, mesmerising, like a dream. And then on the Monday she put me on a bus for San Francisco, and I caught my plane back to Australia that night. I was afraid she would cry when I left, that it would be awkward somehow, but she actually asked me why anyone could be sad after something so beautiful. She said she wanted to remember it for just what it was, and made me promise that I would never try to make contact with her again. Or ever tell anyone about it. And I think I've only ever done so once or twice, in thirty-five years.'

'A story, at last! I was getting so *bored* with philosophy! And charming, too. Two nights and a day! I don't see why it can't be like that more often. But I'm not sure that it's really a cutting of the knot. She sounds as if she was wise, but it might also be that she was just very good at protecting herself. Another day, another night, another week, and it might not have been possible. For me, I have not often been so lucky.'

'"Not often"? So it has happened?'

'Yes, but maybe not quite as you might think.'

'How do you mean?'

'Well, for a start it is not about a man but about a woman, a girl. And also because, I don't know, it might not really be about the knot. It's just that something about your story, the innocence of it, reminded me.'

'Maybe that has something to do with it. Innocence. Youth. When things are more possible. When *more* things are possible. Experience changes us. I've seen it embitter so many people, make them more cautious. You accumulate responsibilities. There is more and more at risk. And less and less time to recover from one's losses . . .

'So?' He wanted to move on.

'So?'

'Your story.' Smiling. 'It's my turn to be told a story.'

'Okay. Yes. The story. I feel like I should say "Once upon a time"! But yes, okay. When we had finished our examinations in high school – there is this sort of tradition here, of going on a trip with your schoolfriends when, although some teachers come with you to make sure you don't get into too much trouble, you have ten days or so when you are free, can experiment, go a little wild.'

'And you experimented? with a friend?'

'No, it wasn't like that. She was not really even my friend, this girl. I knew her and had always liked her – we were always friendly toward one another – but we were in different classes and there had been no special connection. I had a boyfriend in my own class, Paolo, who had been in love with me for two or three years although nothing had ever happened, and she had a boyfriend too, and I think each of us had been looking forward to being with them. We were on a ship, a ferry, here on the Adriatic. We sailed from Venice and went down to Greece, to Ios, stayed there for five days and then sailed back. And on the trip down and all the time on the island it was wonderful . . . the freedom and the fun and the food, the partying, the drinking. But with the boys it was more difficult. I had always found the boys of my own age rather stupid. Too eager and too ignorant, too unpredictable, so insecure that they seemed always to be having to prove themselves. The only real sexual relationship I had had up until that point was with an older man, and I was still seeing him. In a way I had been spoilt, but that's another story. For this trip I was with Paolo. I guess I was caught up in the excitement of it, and perhaps I was enjoying making the older man a little jealous. And I suppose I also thought – I was so sophisticated in my own mind! – that I could teach Paolo something.

'But as I say it was difficult. We had a great time partying but when we went to bed, although it could be very sweet and affectionate when he wasn't desperately trying to show how male he was, it was not very successful. I think eventually I kind of froze him out.'

'Froze him out?'

'Yes. Just went dead. It wasn't that I lost all interest, but I couldn't bring myself to do anything to encourage him. I have always recalled it to myself as if I were looking at him, as he struggled on with whatever he was doing, from a sort of great distance, as though he were some kind of very large insect. I can't see that any man would find that very arousing. And his erection, if he had one in the first place, would just disappear, and there would be nothing he could do to get it back. Poor Paolo. It must have been awful, to have been watched like that. I guess he felt more and more ridiculous, and more and more angry, but I couldn't help it. There was nothing I could do. It was as if my body wouldn't follow my orders.

'By the time we were back on board the ship on the way home, he was no longer coming to my cabin, and to cover it he was drinking and partying too much and passing out. This girl, Graziella, might have been having a similar experience. I don't know. I hadn't been paying much attention, though I had certainly had the impression that she and her boyfriend were getting along well and doing all the things at night that they might have been expected to.'

The waiter came, took away the salad bowl and their side plates, the cutlery, and asked if they would like dessert. She was deep in her story – they both were – and he sensed that she asked to see the list as much to be left alone again as out of any particular interest. They waited a few moments for him to return with the menus. A bell somewhere off in the deepening blue of the night struck nine, and a few seconds later the fountain burst into life. The whole piazza seemed to surge for a moment. But it was a passing thing, a chimera. After little more than a minute the fountain stopped. The waiter, returning, said that there had been problems with it all spring. No one could explain why it would do that, turn on for a few seconds, then stop again for hours. Council workers had been out to try to fix it but so far nothing had been achieved. Maybe it was some problem out under the piazza somewhere, too complicated to do anything about before the tourist season, or maybe it was a hitch with a computer. No doubt the council would fix it, as usual, at the time it would cause the greatest inconvenience.

'So?' he said, prompting her, once the waiter had gone.

'On the last night I had gone to bed early. The partying and the very late nights – several times we had not gone to bed before dawn – were too much for me. I also didn't very much like having to watch Paolo get so drunk.

'I had been reading for a while, enjoying the sound of the ship's motors – it is a beautiful sound, it seems to echo out in the water somewhere – and had fallen asleep. I don't know what time it was when I was woken by knocking on my cabin door. I thought it was Paolo and called out to him to go away, but it continued. I got annoyed and went to the door ready to snap his head off, but it was Graziella. Her boyfriend had fallen asleep on her bed very drunk and was snoring and she couldn't wake him, and someone else was in his cabin having sex so she couldn't go there. When she had discovered that and come back to her own cabin determined to wake her boyfriend and throw him out she found the door locked. She had no idea how it had happened, and she didn't have the key. It was some silly sick trick of his, perhaps, or maybe he had thought that he was in his own cabin, but now she was in her nightdress and locked out and didn't know what to do. She asked if she could sleep on my floor. She was crying, though probably more out of frustration than anything, and even trembling, though it wasn't cold. I let her in. I didn't know what else to do.

'She calmed down after a while, and we started to talk. About the stupidity of boys at first, and their awkwardness, but then about many other things, until very late. Eventually we made up a kind of bed on the floor beside my bunk with the spare pillow and spare blanket and I went back to sleep. But I was woken – it was more a sort of half-woken – some time later by the most warm and amazing feelings, erotic feelings, and I realised that it was Graziella, you know, lying beside me, making love to me, touching my breasts, caressing my neck, stroking me, and for some reason – it felt so good, and was so gentle, after all Paolo's awkwardness – there was no desire to stop her. And then we made love for what seemed like hours before eventually she went back to the bed on the floor. It was a little like you said, mesmerising, a kind of dream.

'When I woke up again – it was late, and I had missed breakfast – she was gone. And when we encountered each other later in the day we were caught up in the business of disembarking. She was in a different carriage of the train on the way home. When I saw her at the station she was with her boyfriend, but she gave me the most beautiful, secret smile. And that was the last I ever saw of her. We had not agreed that we would never have contact or anything like that, but we never did. It's almost as if each of us had decided to seal the experience off, just as it had been, and not let anything subsequent disturb it.'

'You've not had a repeat – a similar experience?'

'You mean have I had sex with another woman? Am I a lesbian? No. Not really. I thought I might be, I wondered, but although I think I may be bisexual – I think probably everyone is bisexual in some measure – and I did try it again, it was only a trial and it just proved to me that what had happened with Graziella was something different and special. This time, this second time, it was all quite deliberate. I went to a lesbian bar, and picked someone up, but when it came to the physical act – and she was very tender, too, this second woman – there was no real feeling, no real desire. It was just a kind of acting. And I froze her out just as I had Paolo. There was no *necessity* to it, there wasn't any particular attraction. I didn't need *her*; I just wanted to try *it*. And I realised that the night with Graziella had had something about it that couldn't be found in this way. With Graziella it was spontaneous, unexpected, completely unplanned.'

They paused, smiled, made eye contact. Each of them, it seemed to him, trying to search the other, or perhaps just for the next thing to say. A late arrival at the restaurant – a large man in a business suit, looking exhausted, distracted – squeezed past them on his way to the one remaining table. They each moved their seats slightly, then shifted them back.

'And the older man?' he said, wanting more story.

'I'll come to him, but first, I want to ask you, how do you feel about that idea that I just mentioned, that everyone is bisexual? I mean, maybe there is no *actual*, *natural* gender limitation at all, maybe that's only cultural. Perhaps the only reason that people don't know that they're actually bisexual is that they haven't experienced it with the right people, and because society is always sending this constant message that they should be heterosexual, that it is only that that is normal. It's like, as we've been saying, a lot of people don't ever get to sleep with somebody they're deeply attracted to, and they just take what is available to them. So?'

'So?'

'So what about you? Are you bisexual? Have you ever slept with a man, or been deeply attracted to one?'

He was taken aback. It wasn't a kind of question he was used to contemplating, let alone one he might have been expecting. 'No,' he said, stumbling a little. 'No, I can't say that I have. I mean, I have never slept with a man, or ever felt the desire to.'

'That sounds like an automatic answer to me. Are you sure about that? Never? At all?'

'Yes. I'm quite sure. I don't want to rule out your idea entirely. It actually seems quite plausible.

121

But the cultural conditioning is very strong, as you say, that pressure to be heterosexual, and perhaps in me it's been too strong to allow anything else through. My interests – my desires – have always been heterosexual. I think the closest I might ever have come would have been an exaggerated admiration for some older kid or another when I was a boy, but it never occurred to me then or since that it was sexual. It was a long time before I even knew what that was. It was just a matter of *cool*, of someone I wanted to emulate, someone I thought I wanted to be like. On one occasion,' suddenly remembering, smiling, relaxing a little, 'it was largely a matter of a motorcycle.'

'A motorcycle?'

'Yes, when I was maybe eleven or twelve. An American, travelling around Australia on a motorcycle, eighteen or nineteen he might have been, maybe a bit older. And for some reason he ended up in our driveway. I've no idea why. But he was there, in his leather jacket and his spiky blond hair, with this big, gleaming, blue-and-silver motorcycle. I don't remember whether he stayed with us overnight or was just there for a morning, but it's a shining image and was certainly some kind of intense crush for me, though whether for him or for his motorcycle I just couldn't say. In my memory they're inextricable.'

'Did he take you for a ride on it? That throbbing engine between your thighs?' She was smiling again.

'I can't remember! Honestly. Surely, if he had, I would have some clearer recollection. Perhaps my parents forbade it. Later though, six or seven years later, I did get a motorcycle of my own.'

'Big and silver and blue?'

'No. Red. And not very big. A 250cc. Honda. Enough for me. And you? Have you ever had a motorcycle?'

'No, not of my own, but I have ridden them, been taken on them,' and here it seemed something unpleasant crossed her mind; he could almost feel her pushing it away. Body language, eye language: the way she glared, momentarily, at the tea-candle.

'So,' she said, looking up, 'nothing since the American boy? No friends you have been particularly drawn to?'

'No, not in that way. Not sexually. In Australia we have a famous tradition of *mateship*, a kind of machismo, I guess it is, a bond between men, that has a lot to do with work and common experience and drinking. It has some virtues of loyalty, but at the same time can be a kind of complicity, a kind of conspiracy to overlook one another's faults. And we also have a great tradition of sports in which men come into intimate contact with one another, like a kind of institutionalised bisexuality. But I've never been very good at either of them, the mateship or the sport. My real friends have always been women. I've always felt I could talk more intimately, be more myself with women.'

'No male intimates then? Surely there have been men with whom you have been able to talk intimately.'

'Not often, and not in the terms I was just thinking of, of opening myself to them. There were a couple of friends at university, one in particular, with whom it seemed I could share just about anything, but that was as much a matter of drugs and so forth. A lot of marijuana, a lot of music, many late nights, a lot of hitch-hiking around the country together.' Tosh. Bozic. Should he go there? No. 'But since then almost nobody. Especially in the last twenty years or so. It's not, to be honest, that I haven't wanted it sometimes, and haven't found men with whom I would have liked to have close friendships – men I've imagined might be my best friends, if I were able to have them.'

'If you were able to have them?'

'Somehow it's never seemed to work out. Either they are too far away, or too busy in their careers, or I let my own career get in the way, never follow through, as if I have a tic of some sort, something inside me that won't let them happen, that chokes them off before they really get started.'

'Perhaps Freud would have something to say about that.' She smiled. 'The suppression of a bisexual urge. The awkwardness about, what did you call it? mateship? The avoidance of the contact sports. The choking off of friendships.'

'Ah, the game of opposites! If I order red wine it's because I really want white. If I order fish it's because I want pork. If I say I don't want male friendships it's because I really desire them. No. You *may* be right, of course, but I don't think it's as simple as that.'

He had answered testily, a loss of patience, and was surprised at himself, hoped that it had not been noticeable. But of course it had, and she changed the subject.

'But I interrupted you,' she said, 'earlier, when we were talking about Graziella. What were you asking?'

He had to think about it for a moment. 'I imagine I was asking about the older man. You said you were having a relationship with an older man, at around the same time as you had your experience with Graziella.'

'He was a school teacher. My Italian teacher. We started an affair early in my final year of high school. He was very caring, gave me gifts, made me feel mature, and he was an excellent lover who taught me a great deal and got me very interested in sex for a time, even a little addicted. I think that, technically, it was probably pederasty, since it began when I was sixteen, but it never felt like that. In fact I did all I could, over several months, to attract him. He was married and had two small children. We used to meet in a house he had inherited in a village about ten kilometres away from my own.

'I was in love with him, and he said that he was in love with me, and I thought that love gave us a kind of divine right to be together whatever the cost. Then one day perhaps two weeks after high school had finished – two weeks after the trip to Greece, when I had so desperately wanted him to be one of the teachers who came with us, but he wasn't – I met him by accident at a shopping centre. He was with his wife and children. This lovely, soft woman. He introduced me as he would introduce any other student in his class. And he fled, like a coward, and left me with her. She asked me if I would like some coffee and we talked, not about him, of course, but other things. And I liked her! I mean *really* liked her, although up until then I had made her in my mind into a kind of witch. She was warm, and gentle, and strong, and very beautiful. She put one of the children in my lap, for me to hold, the most beautiful girl! And after that I not only started to hate him, but started to think about her. That was one of the reasons I tried something with a second woman. The way I found myself feeling about his wife. I might almost have transferred my affections to her. I had to make sure somehow, but not with her. His wife! That is what

I mean about being a dangerous woman, I think. So changeable, and careless about consequences. Certainly I was a dangerous girl.'

'It sounds as if he was a dangerous man, if a bit sad and pathetic too. Lost.' This said with a pang. 'But the consequences, you know, are also not always entirely your own responsibility. Everything we do, every relationship we have, involves at least two. The other person is there also. And in this case each of them, the husband – and the wife, had you had that relationship with her that you fantasised about – were much older than you.'

'Ten years. It doesn't seem so much now, ten years later, when I'm the age they were then. But I suppose you are right. I suppose I have always seen these relationships as coming from my own initiative – certainly I've planned some of them, taken the initiative – when of course there were always two.

'But you were saying something else . . .' She seemed to want to pass the baton, though for the moment, the waiter having approached, it hung in the air.

Had they decided about dessert?

'Yes,' she began, making eye contact across the

table to confirm, 'I mean, dessert would be nice, but later perhaps. I am still hungry. And I want to keep talking. And I am enjoying the wine. Let us have something else first?'

'Cheese?' Stephen remembered. 'Would you like some cheese?'

'Yes, *formaggi*. And a little more *teran*. Another pitcher, a half-litre, or maybe just an extra glass, since I am driving.' He asked the waiter about the cheeses – did they have gorgonzola? and some others, a selection. And ordered another half-litre. There was, after all, no compulsion to finish it. And they would keep the menus, let him know about dessert later. In this brief break in the conversation he looked around him. A group of Chinese tourists was crossing the square – perhaps after having dinner in one of the Chinese restaurants he had seen earlier in the day on the other side of the Canal Grande – two-by-two behind a young man carrying a white flag on a stick. Across the restaurant from them, at the table that had been marked *Riservato*, the elderly couple were eating slowly, with small, meticulous movements, still not saying a word.

'Do you mind if I smoke?' she asked after the

waiter had gone. 'Do you smoke? I don't smoke a lot, but I like to sometimes, after a meal. Especially outdoors like this.'

'No, I don't mind at all. I know how you feel. I used to smoke. I don't any more, but I still enjoy it vicariously. Do you need cigarettes?'

'No, I have some. But I do need an ashtray.' He moved to signal the waiter but she stopped him, put her hand on his wrist, indicated that there was an ashtray on the next table. She got up and fetched it for herself, then took out a soft silver pack of a cigarette he hadn't seen before, lit one, and blew the first draw of smoke slowly into the air above them. His daughter Anne would have been disgusted – a shower of carcinogenic particles, she would have said, a bombardment of poison – but the scent, for the moment, was delicious.

FORMAGGI

———————————

'Something else?' He was drawing her back to whatever it had been that she had been drawing him back to, although he himself couldn't remember. They had talked about so much.

'Something else . . . Ah, yes, back before I made you tell your story about the girl in the college room. You were saying that you have sometimes thought you were incapable of loving.'

'Yes,' he remembered now, 'but then there have been other times when I've been so eviscerated, so utterly devastated that I've not been in any doubt at all.'

'"Eviscerated"?'

'Yes, gutted, as they do in a slaughterhouse – those horrible places – when they cut open the body and all of the innards fall out. A huge over-statement, but it does sometimes feel like that.'

'If we can ever begin to imagine what that must be like,' staring into the air above him, then forcing herself back. 'But these times of yours, when you felt something like that. Tell me about them.'

'No, I . . .'

'Tell me!' Dismay in her voice, and sternness. 'We have already agreed upon this. You cannot at one point say that the marvellous thing about conversations with strangers is that you can say anything to them and then as soon as it comes to it, how do you say this? You close up, like a *clam*.' She smiled, as if pleased to have found the word.

'Well, my mother's death, for one. I was young, nineteen, and although at the time I went numb, in a way, and even thought I was somehow abnormal for not feeling anything, I think in truth I was grieving for years.'

'Your mother? The swimmer? Oh no. I am sorry! So young! And after such a romantic beginning! Oh, I am so sorry! But of course you mentioned before that your mother had died. And your father – how did he take such a thing?'

'He was devastated. Empty, you know, shocked, threw himself into his job – became a kind of workaholic in fact. But it's strange how history repeats itself. About ten years afterward he met another woman, and they married a couple of years later. My brother and sister seemed to deal with it fairly well, but I don't think I did. I never got along with her, my stepmother. And my father and I, well, we weren't exactly estranged, but there was a kind of awkwardness, a stiffness, for years.'

'Like he had been with his own father.'

'Yes. Not nearly as bad as that. But yes. That's what I mean: history repeating itself.'

'But that resentment of the new woman is normal, I think, or at least not unusual. And anyway a mother's death – and forgive me for this; I don't mean to be disrespectful – doesn't really count. Of course one is eviscerated, but it's not the kind of relationship we have been talking about.'

'No, but it carries over, into relationships you have afterward.'

'You think so? Yes, I suppose it would. Then we truly *are* out of our own control, aren't we? Sorry. As I said, I did not intend to be dismissive.

But tell me, please, about the other times . . . if they are not too painful.'

'My first wife, for one. I haven't mentioned her yet. Before Carol. We were almost children, it now seems to me, married straight out of university and not really ready for such a thing. Certainly I wasn't. I was barely twenty-two, and she was a month or two younger than me. We were hippies together. It was a time of free love, supposedly, but actually very confused. The marriage lasted six years or so. I had a few affairs. I didn't really see them like that at the time, but I realised soon enough that that is what they were. I think she – Jane, her name was Jane – must have known, though she never said and I never told her. And then she fell in love herself, with a visiting English musician, a member of a famous rock band.'

'And she left you for him?'

'No. It didn't happen quite that way. We came to Europe, on a holiday. I had got a small inheritance, from that English aunt I mentioned, otherwise we could never have afforded it. It was something we'd been planning for a while – the big trip abroad – though I realised that for her it had become so that she could see him. I guess I felt guilty about my affairs and that I owed it to her somehow. But all this was more or less unspoken. Now, in hindsight, it seems amazing that we could have left so much unspoken, but that's the way it was. And we did go to see him. We were in England for two weeks. He was living in a boathouse on a river. The River Dart, I think it was. We had a rented car and we drove there.'

'You drove her to him . . .'

'Yes, literally as well as figuratively. The last mile was along a track right beside the river, and about halfway along we had to stop to rescue a ewe – a sheep – that had become stuck in the mud on the riverbank. And then we drove on, and I said hello to the musician briefly then went for a long walk, to give them some time.'

'What? To make love or something?'

'I don't know. Certainly I thought that was what was happening. I walked for I think nearly two hours, further along the river. It probably wasn't more than two hours, perhaps a lot less, but it felt like an eternity. In a kind of agony. I felt I was being punished for my own unfaithfulness.'

'You were punishing yourself! But that is such a strange story. Like something out of *Possession*.

Or a painting by one of those Victorian English painters. Rossetti? The sheep, the boathouse, the muddy road, the walk in agony. So this was your evisceration?'

'No. Not really. Or yes, the first part of it. I do think that something broke then – that she and I were not ever really comfortable with one another after that – but the real blow was still to come. We struggled on for a couple of years, back in Sydney, and then I got a job on the other side of Australia, a big career opportunity for me, with one of the mining companies, and she did not want to come. I couldn't blame her. It was only a one-year contract and I hoped that we could manage it long-distance, but after a few months, when we had only seen each other two or three times, she said that she had started a relationship with someone else, and wanted a trial separation, to see what happened with this other person. And then everything fell apart for me. I suddenly realised what I had lost. I roamed the streets late at night, in that outback town, out on the edge of the desert, for nearly a week, sobbing and howling and raving to myself. People must have thought I had gone mad.'

'It does sound a bit disproportionate, but maybe it was a kind of double grief. Maybe you were grieving for your mother at last.'

'I think that's probably exactly right! I had never thought of it that way! In all this time! But I think you're right. Thank you.'

'It's only your own point. About one grief influencing others. I just gave it back to you.

'How old were you when this happened?'

'Twenty-nine or thirty by then. Just a bit older than you.'

'And what about the musician?'

'The musician? I don't know. Jane swore blind that nothing occurred that afternoon. That they hadn't made love or anything, just talked. And of course I didn't believe her, though I pretended to. Now I'm not so sure. I think she might just have been telling the truth. Things went quiet after that. He was hardly mentioned. I guess it's one thing to have a bit of a fling while you're visiting Australia, but quite another when that fling turns up on your doorstep, with a husband wandering about in the woods outside. Quite weird, when you think about it. Probably he backed right off.'

'And then? for you?'

'Then? Well, then I recovered, slowly, but recovered, as it seems I always do.'

'You said there were other times. Other, what did you call them? Guttings? Mortifications?'

'Well, yes. *An*other.' He'd thought of others, but pushed them away. The night was beautiful. No place for recriminations. 'But I will tell you only on the condition that you will tell me something also, about your own eviscerations.'

'Yes, certainly. Anything. Almost! But only if I am satisfied with what you tell to me now.'

The waiter brought the cheese, three pieces, a large flat tranche of gorgonzola, a wedge of a harder cheese, pecorino of some kind, and a small half-wheel of something softer, a *chèvre*? And cherries, and some fine slices of apple arranged like a fan. A basket of biscuits with four small rolls of dark bread. And the wine. They hardly paused in their conversation.

'A woman I met on a beach, in a town on the coast north of Sydney. Two or three years after that marriage. I don't really think it would be fair to call it an evisceration. Others might call it a tragedy, but

I still don't know what to call it. It left me feeling so helpless, so hollow. I was back working in Sydney, freshly divorced and freshly in from the desert, a bit lost. A friend took me to see this woman when I was up visiting him. I don't think he was trying to set us up or anything like that. They were friends and he admired her, thought she was wonderful and wanted me to meet her. But almost immediately there was an extraordinary connection between us. At least I thought there was. She was about four or five years older than me, and had a house on the beach, on a headland, overlooking the ocean. She was very sad. Her husband had been killed, washed off the rocks while fishing – a freak wave – and drowned, a year before. It happens quite often on that coast. I visited her several times in the week I was there, and then over the next few months came up every weekend or two. We were starting to have a relationship: nothing physical, though I was certainly keen for it, but she was wary, afraid to be hurt again. And there was always this deep sadness that I couldn't penetrate. We would go for long walks on the beach. Or she would come to dinner at my friend's house up in the town and I would walk her back.

'Eventually, though, something did happen. I came up from Sydney to stay at my friend's place, it may have been for the fifth or sixth time, and she seemed lighter, happier somehow. I had the feeling something had changed, that the grief had receded a little. She said she would like to cook me a meal. I took some nice wine and – ', pausing, wondering if there were any way he could get out of this now, stop the telling.

'And?' She would not have pushed, probably, had he explained, but then the only explanation was the thing itself.

'And, well, it was a beautiful evening. And she was, I don't know, *radiant*, so much happier than I'd seen her before. We sat on the veranda and watched the night come in over the sea, and ate, and drank the wine . . .'

'Much like this night.'

'Yes, much like this night, though instead of a huge marble-paved piazza with shining cutlery and starched tablecloths and a church-bell ringing the hours there was the breeze in the spotted gums and the sound of possums and the crashing of surf.

'And we did, eventually, make love. And I didn't feel that I was pushing her. I felt that she was as keen as I. And it was beautiful. Full of the night breeze and the ringing dark,' yes, that was at last the word for it, the *ringing* dark, 'and she came, but then she sobbed, and sobbed, deep, wrenching sobs, so that I thought – it was clear enough – that the grief had caught up with her, flooded back when she thought that perhaps she had outpaced it. I tried to comfort her but it didn't work and when she'd recovered a little, barely, she asked me to go. She apologised, you know? She was so gracious and almost loving about it, but she asked me to go and it seemed to me that that was the right thing to do, the only thing to do.'

'Of course. What else could you have done?' She searched his eyes.

'Yes, but then, the next morning . . . I had hardly slept, it was such a long sad night, thinking about her, and about my own sadnesses, my own griefs, as if hearing and encountering hers, that new level of it, had somehow opened up my own. And the next morning I showered and dressed and walked back down the beach toward her house.'

'Oh no . . .' She knew it already, could hear it in his voice.

'I could see a group of people at her end of

the beach, and vehicles. It didn't take me long to work out that they were police and an ambulance. I didn't even run. I just had this horrible, eerie certainty. She was lying just above the tide-line, with a dark blanket pulled over her face. They wouldn't let me near her or up to the house. They worked out pretty quickly that I must've been the last person to see her alive, and they questioned me extensively, on and off for days, in fact, while they were waiting for the autopsy report. I thought for a while that they were going to charge me. But my friend knew when I'd come in and she'd died much later, near dawn, and eventually they lost interest in me. When the report came it didn't suggest any crime. The coroner's conclusion was quite unequivocally that it was suicide. The inquest was a formality. But I struggled for years with the thought that I had contributed somehow. That I *had* pushed her, for my own desire, my own needs, and hadn't seen.'

'You blamed yourself? Yes, I suppose that is natural. But I imagine you were no more to blame than she was to blame for her husband's death, or than he was for dying, or than the sea for sweeping him off the rocks. I don't really think that we are agents – is it "agents" or "agencies"? – as often as we think we are. You could think of it differently. That in a way she was using you, maybe without any idea that that was what she was doing, to take her to a place she would have trouble getting to otherwise, but that she needed to go to. And that she had to trust you, maybe even love you, in order to let you take her there. Maybe *that* was the explanation of her radiance. And the way you describe it, you know, it was a beautiful night.' He had been looking at the wrinkles on the back of his hands, around the knuckles, at the base of his thumb, fingering the stem of his wine glass, thinking of the long beach, but looked up, at Irena with her striking grey eyes, holding his look so firmly, then out, at the dark square.

The night, in its inscrutable arrangements, had chosen this moment to place a pair of young men on the edge of the silent fountain, youths he might have expected to be playing soccer somewhere, dribbling the ball with dancers' lightness, passing it to one another with uncanny accuracy, taking it on the chest and holding it there without hands;

not, as the one was clearly doing, weeping, or, as was the other, stroking his friend's cheek with such tenderness.

They found that they had both been watching them, surreptitiously – how had that happened? one instant the beach, the strangeness of his fingers, the next this – and turned again to the cheese, in shared embarrassment. And after some moments, not even a minute, the boys left, walking away in separate directions, the one who had not cried, after twenty metres or so, turning around, walking backward for five, six paces, watching the back of his friend, then turning again, running off. Was he going home? Was he going to meet someone else?

The gorgonzola was sharp, strong, pungent, ammoniac, its intense concentration of flavour somehow precipitous, poised deliciously on the edge of a kind of rottenness. And then the *teran*, when he took a small draught of it, cutting through it, now almost sweet by comparison, altering it, balancing it. He tilted his glass slightly, looking into the extraordinary colour of the wine. He had never seen such a rich, deep garnet. The sheer intensity of it seemed to revive him, as if he had glimpsed something through it, in it, blood-like, that coursed through everything.

'You know, the way we were talking of pain, a little while ago, and whether it had a kind of necessary connection with love?' – this was her, as it happened, though for a second could have been either of them, since their thoughts had formed, momentarily, a confluence. 'I'm wondering if there might be another reason why love seems such a painful thing for some people, something almost to be feared. Because they are afraid of losing something, of being diminished somehow, of relinquishing control of the situation or of themselves. Or because they have to let go of something they have been holding onto so tightly.'

'Holding onto so tightly? What do you mean?'

'I mean it's so hard, for all of us, isn't it? to make ourselves into separate, independent beings in the first place, to become adult, to establish our borders, our edges, and then, you know, love can seem like you have to open those borders, maybe almost as soon as you've got them.'

'Or got them back . . . Yes, I guess so. You were saying that before. That's why trust is so much a part of it, so important, for so many. So how come it's so easy for others, do you think?'

'I don't know. Maybe that kind of identity isn't so important to them. Or maybe they're more confident in themselves, less afraid that they are going to be diminished. Maybe they have more of themselves to give. Maybe they haven't had such a battle getting themselves together in the first place.'

'So that love's a kind of privilege? I mean the kind that involves pleasure that way – that it's an ability that's given by circumstance, or created by circumstance?' The idea, after all, did seem quite similar to something he'd been saying earlier.

'I don't know about privilege, but certainly one is fortunate to find something like that. Have you?' she looked at him almost earnestly now. 'Ever?'

'Yes,' he said, 'I have, at last, in Genevieve, but it's been a long time in coming.'

'And yet you might never have got there.'

'"Never have got there"? How do you mean?'

'A lot of people might have got stuck somewhere along the way, might never have reached such a place.'

'And yet the way was full of error and damage,

and deceit.' He seemed to be admitting something, to himself, and stifled a shudder.

'Yes, I think that is what I was implying.'

'So strange, that there can be a kind of, I don't know, *reward*, after all that. But that, I suppose,' the thought had suddenly struck him, 'is to assume that the world works the way we've always been taught that it does, and perhaps it doesn't.'

And with that, reluctantly, had had to excuse himself. In need of a urinal. And soon returned, having had a further thought there, while staring at the glistening porcelain tiles. One of those rare glimpses of structure and clarity, it had seemed, that are sent to tease us with the possibility that we might be other than we are. But then had lost it, some vital part of it – it had slipped through his fingers – in the sudden access of light and crystal, the gleaming silverware, the shining mirrors, the crisp whiteness of napery in the restaurant's interior, and the view of her, her back half-turned to him, sitting alone at the table. But he was grasping for it, and would still try.

'You know,' he said, when he had settled again

and looked out over the square, gathering himself for this new territory, 'in the dark, when you are really lovers – in the dark or the light, it doesn't matter – it can be almost Dantescan and – '

'Dantescan? How do you mean? Paradise? The Inferno? Purgatory?'

'I mean all three! It's often seemed to me that I've had bits of all of them, in the same day, the same hour! And that that is normal, surely, is the way life is. But it's mainly an atmosphere I'm thinking of when I say Dantescan, rich and visceral, intense, poetic, full of the spirit and states of the spirit.' He suspected this wouldn't satisfy her; it didn't satisfy him; and yet Dante, when he'd read him, had been a world, *the* world.

'I suppose I should just have said *so invested with meaning*, and yet at the same time, in the dark like that, in the throes of loving, it's all also so deeply primitive. You are eating one another almost, tasting, smelling, entering, with fingers, tongues, minds, with your memory, with your hopes, with your appetite, as if you are both, together, the one creature, the one being that is seeking itself, but will also never be satisfied until it has swallowed itself somehow.'

'Like Uroboros, that snake that swallows its own tail.'

'Yes, like that, a snake's not a bad image for it. And it goes on, it seems as if it *wants* to go on, until the very end of things, illness, death. As if love, desire, were some huge force that we're only on the margins of.'

'Something that will devour us.'

'Yes, something that will devour us. Or that we are caught up by, and that dumps us when it's finished with us.'

'I don't know. That all makes sense, but there's a kind of warning bell going off in my head.'

'A warning bell?'

'Yes, on the one hand that's all so *male*' – her hand moved, as if to touch his wrist, to prepare him for something, but withdrew – 'You know: the woman as darkness, the man pressing in on a voyage of discovery.' He was about to interject – *ob*ject – but she would not let him. 'And you will probably protest that you are talking about both male *and* female here, but that is part of the problem, that the male thinks – assumes, automatically, so often – that what *he* is experiencing *she* is experiencing also. Isn't it just as likely, when the man

feels that they are eating each other and all that –
what did you say? that they are one creature? – that
the female feels something very different? That she
is being entered, say, invaded? I'm not saying that
I feel this way, but I know that others do – that
Claudia does, for example: brutalised somehow,
subjected.'

'But I'm speaking about lovers . . .'

'How can you ever be sure? Maybe the man
speaks about "making love" because he *wants*
to, and the woman only talks about it that way
because she *has* to. But even that's not right,
not really what I want to say. Probably it's too
extreme, sounds too brutal.' Again he was about
to interject, but she was on the verge of something
and waved his comment away. 'But even that, the
fact that I can't really, very easily, say what I want
to say, is part of it, almost as if all the words we're
using are stiff, awkward, ill-fitting. And it's not
just because we are speaking in English, which
is still a little strange and difficult for me, even
after so much practice and study. It is like that in
Italian too.

'And yet in another way you're right, we
are devoured, but even in this there's a crucial

difference. *Your* devourment – can I use that word, devourment? – is conceptual, but for women it has been, for so long, terribly real. We're getting over it a little now, perhaps, but for most of human history "making love" could be a kind of death sentence, or at least a very high-risk activity, in all sorts of ways. Probably, with you, I don't need to list them.'

'No, maybe not. You know, in a way – even if it's a kind of male way, which for the moment I'm not sure how I can get around – that is not too far from the point I was getting at. I think we may be agreeing as much as we are disagreeing.'

'Perhaps, and I should let you finish your point. I did interrupt.'

'No. Please. I enjoy and appreciate the contradiction. I am probably full of presumptions and brutalities – in fact I know I am – but that doesn't mean I want to keep them or defend them. What would be the point in that? If I've learnt anything in these centuries of mine it's that that kind of pride is a bit stupid. It would be so good to break out of all that, and step free. To be able to talk openly, without the . . .' He paused, not so much looking for the word, as surprised, at last, to have found it, to be seeing it so clearly.

'Without the what?'

'The shadow, I think you could call it. Without the shadow. That sense that everything one says in certain areas – in the most important areas – might be a violation, some kind of error. Men, I think, have also come to feel that language betrays them.'

She looked at him quizzically. Had what he'd said surprised her, or was it just that she wasn't quite sure of what she'd heard? He could see her about to make a comment, but then back away. She picked up the knife, as if to cut a last piece of the pecorino, then put it down again.

'So?' she asked. 'What *were* you in the process of saying, when I kidnapped the conversation? And you can speak freely, without fear of violating, or violation.' She smiled. Was it irony? Sarcasm? No. Not even amusement. Affection. Friendship. 'Language is all we have, after all, so we have to use it.'

He felt so foolish, starting again, but that was pride also.

Having, to gather his mind, taken a few moments to force his own knife through what remained of the harder cheese, then place the thin slice on a cracker – he waded in, the cheese and the cracker momentarily untouched.

'Love is the hardest thing, you know? Everyone turns their back on it, the philosophers and the theologians especially, in defeat, I guess, or disappointment.'

'Or fear, I suppose, if it's going to devour us. You'd turn your back out of a sense of survival.'

'No, I think it's more that they know their true enemy. It is so human, the deepest, hardest human – the *ground* of the human – the ground zero of being.'

'As much as death itself?'

'Yes, I'd say so. Just as much, since it's to do with procreation in the first place: the bringing into life that is, what would you call it? the *counterweight* of death? and at the same time the beginning of dying, a death sentence. And the philosophers, the theologians, the Church, especially the Church, have to elevate it, sublimate it, because only there and then, without these human things on their hands – blood, cum, semen, sweat, shit, vomit – can they cauterise it, control it.'

'You are a mystic, I think, and a sensualist at the same time.' She smiled. '"Dantescan".'

'By which you mean you don't agree? or that I'm not expressing myself very well?'

'A little of both, perhaps, but more of the former', she said, still smiling. 'I'm not sure that that is really the way they see it, the Church. I don't know about philosophers and theologians, but I have spent a lot of my life amongst priests. It is Italy, after all. And I am sure that some of them would say – the few who know and have thought enough, and don't feel, as so many of them seem to feel, that they have to talk to their parishioners as if they were children as inexperienced as they themselves are – that it's more as if there is a kind of emptiness in us, at our core, a need or vacancy that we try to fill with each other, and that all that business, what did you say? the blood, the semen, the sweat? – the sex, but then we do this just as effectively to each other emotionally, without sex – is just our devouring each other, our gnawing each other, trying to get through each other, to the bones, to find that missing thing that might make us whole. But that thing is not there, you can't ever find it. Perhaps it's just that the philosophers and theologians know

154

that the search is futile, that you can't ever find, here, in that way, anything that can fill that emptiness. That the emptiness is essential to us, part of us, and that the only thing that can fill it – this is certainly what the priests would say – is God.'

'But that emptiness, surely, is only one way of explaining something. The Church would *have* to explain it as a hole, an absence, something that only God can fill. It's too good an opportunity to miss. And it's not only the Church. What about that idea – I forget whose it is or where I came across it, a long time ago now – that we're caught up in a kind of romantic *economy*?'

'"Romantic economy"?'

'Yes, the argument that at least part of our understanding of what love is is ideological, a whole machinery of myths and stories and beliefs and customs – an avalanche of propaganda! – designed to make us perpetuate the nuclear family and serve the interests at once of patriarchy and, more recently, of an industrialised, consumer society.'

'A way of keeping women in chains. A kind of drug.'

'Right. And not only women. Women predominantly – I think that is without a doubt – but men also. A romantic economy that serves a wider economy. If you are *defined* as a lack, then you're going to need a constant supply of things to fill it.'

'Yes, yes, I understand. It is hard to argue with that. It's almost the point I was making a little while ago, about not being able to *say* some things, because the words were all tainted or inadequate or wrong, or just not there in the first place. Though surely it is more an accumulation over thousands of years, like the way a stalactite is formed, than a product of the Industrial Revolution . . . But even as a woman, you know, I don't think it's adequate to make it exclusively a patriarchal matter. A lot of the things we've been talking about would be common to any society, in one form or another, no matter how primitive or advanced or different it was. The emptiness, the lack, is everywhere; everyone feels it. In a matriarchal society you would feel it probably just as much as in a patriarchal one.'

'Yes, but that's just it. Aren't the lack and emptiness just one way of looking at it? Couldn't we think of the situation differently? I mean, isn't that what we've been trying to do tonight – looking for the moments when we've broken out of the mould somehow? Isn't that what our stories have been about? All that business about cutting the Gordian knot?'

'I'm not sure that I follow you.' She seemed to be searching his eyes.

'Look, an example. I'm an insomniac. Have been, most of my life. Or at least that's the way I'd thought of it. For years. I used to lie awake, getting anxious about all the things I had to do, all the things I hadn't done, desperate for sleep, worried about how I'd be the next morning if I didn't get enough. Thinking of all the wasted time. Until one day I was talking about it with a colleague and she said, Why do you think of it that way? Why not think of it as *given time*? Why not get up, as soon as you realise that you're awake and that you're not going to go back to sleep for a while, and *do* something, so that you might even be *glad* you woke, see it as something *productive*, rather than something wasted. Think of the work you could do, in the quiet, the problems you could solve! So I did. It made such sense. In a small way, it has changed my life. What if the emptiness is like that? Something we could see in a completely different way. Not as a hollow in us that we try so desperately to fill, not even as a lack at all. What if we said to ourselves No, we *are* full already – just redefined it! – and saw desire as something else, not as a sign of our own hollowness, but as something *energising*, a sign of health and vitality?'

'I don't know. That is . . . It is too much. I'm going to have to think about it. It sounds plausible, possible, but I don't know.'

'I probably didn't put that very clearly at all. It's barely clear even to me. But it seems to connect with other things we've been saying. Like there is a constellation in all of this somehow, a deep pattern, if only we knew how to identify it.'

'As if any two people are ever going to be able to solve such questions over dinner, no matter how long and relaxed it is, or how starry the night.' She leant back, took a deep breath. Something to break the intensity. He realised he needed it too.

DOLCE

———— ✦✦✦✦✦✦✦✦✦✦✦✦ ————

They had finished the last of the cheese, and the last drops of *teran*. A few centimetres of the *Lacryma Christi* remained, perhaps half a glass each, in the bottle in the ice bucket, now almost at the same temperature as the night. He asked whether she would like some dessert.

'Yes. I think so. Something light. A *sorbetto*.'

He looked around, caught the waiter's eye. *Sorbetto*, for each of them. Lemon? Yes, lemon.

'And coffee?' he added. 'We might as well do the complete ritual.'

'Yes, but a little later. We don't need to bother about it now. Let us take our time.' Out of nowhere the waiter had produced a crumb brush and swept the table, as if instinctively aware of the rhythms of the conversation, the caesura.

'Do you believe in God, then?' she asked, when the waiter had gone.

'Ah,' he said, and heaved a mock sigh of relief, 'an easy question at last! The answer is No, I don't, and Yes, I do.'

'Pascal's Wager!'

'No, not quite. It's more a No, and a No with a qualification. In other words, No, if we are talking about a maker or creator who has established some system of judgement and good and evil, and who watches or knows us, has some sort of ongoing relationship with us. That god, if he or she or it existed, would have to be resisted at all costs, have to be denied, because history has demonstrated – every single day demonstrates – that *that* being, if it exists, is an unspeakably cruel, even sadistic being, the quintessence of its own definition of evil.'

'Well,' she said, smiling, 'I cannot see much doubt there. So what is the Yes, or the No with the qualification?'

'Let's call it a Yes – if we can accept that such a thing, "God", might just be a kind of mental receptacle, like love and many other things are. Something that exists to be filled by what we think is in it or should be in it.'

'So why would we need it at all then?'

'As a name for things we can't find names for.'

'What sorts of things?'

'Admirations, wonders . . . Also something to fill with the better parts of ourselves, and maybe to goad those better parts into being. Not everyone will need it.'

'Do *you* need it?'

'Not much. There's an old trigger-reflex that wants to think that things have a cause, and to, I don't know, worship, respect that cause, to have some being to thank because of them, because the beauty and the wonder and the, well, you used the term, *mystery*, is too much for us to absorb. But that's an old ghost in the machine, and if I can't seem ever to get rid of it I at least know that that's all it is. And maybe, too, it has some political function.'

'Political . . .'

'Yes, but sad, you know, keeping people in line. Giving them a sense that there's a reward for doing right things, and punishment for doing wrong, because for some pitiful reason most people don't seem to be able to do the right thing on their own initiative, even though, as I strongly believe they do, they have an ingrained sense of what the right things are.'

'So God exists in order to be an authority outside themselves.'

'Yes, that paradox.'

'Another paradox!' She smiled nonchalantly, but was clearly interested.

'Yes, the great one, it seems to me, the paradox of paradoxes, though you never hear anyone talk about it. All these rewards offered in heaven, held out in front of us, and yet any attempt to describe heaven or to give us any sense at all of those rewards is dependent upon things of the earth, things that are *here*, not *there*. We couldn't know anything at all about a *there* even if it existed; we only know *here*, and any account of anything else has to be made up of things *from* here, so that the actual nature of the there is just a cleaned-up, edited version of here, with the nastinesses and confusions taken out. We have spun heaven out of ourselves and our own experience because there is no other way of conceiving anything. Heaven is the glorification of the very earth that we have to deny in order to get to heaven!'

'Lovely. And the idea of God is the same, presumably.'

'Yes?'

'Well, if heaven' – the sorbetto had arrived, in tall, elegant glasses, but she seemed determined to talk on – 'is made out of – is just an edited version of – earth and our earthly experience (and presumably hell is just the same, in the other direction), then couldn't we think of God as something made out of ourselves, in much the same way?'

'Exactly! A vessel to put the best of ourselves in.'

'And the worst of ourselves, too, by your own account. And there is a second level to your paradox, isn't there? A paradox within the paradox. That the rewards being held out in heaven, the rewards that are so inevitably a version of things of this earth, are rewards given for *denying* things of the earth. Especially the kinds of things, the kind of love, we have been talking about.'

'Yes! And there's a further paradox, if I can have one more: that religions tend to perpetuate themselves and their power by rewarding people for avoiding, or punishing them for not avoiding, something, the body, that is deeply part of them, of their essence. You can never avoid your body, except by the most extreme behaviour, and so you're not only always going to be in the wrong – always unredeemed! – but always in a kind of deep confusion, because you're trying to explain and live and understand with a disastrously *edited* version of yourself.

'We'll never really solve any of the major problems of our existence while we pretend to be what we are not, or to be only half of what we are: we need to take the whole of experience, experience as much as we *can* experience, not only so that we know what we are truly dealing with, but because that *is* what we are. This mess of our being is something that has to be *lived through*. The only real wisdom that can ever help us will have come from that, not from avoiding it on the advice of others, who, if they have lived through anything, have only lived through their version of it.'

Something had got into him. An old argument with the world, and it seemed he had had to explain it again. But surely he was in serious danger of boring her, if he wasn't doing so already.

He watched her eating her sorbetto, the way she held the spoon, her slender fingers, her even cuticles, her unblemished nails. Then realised his own was melting in the glass. 'We should do right,' he added, it might almost have been to himself, as he took a first spoonful, 'and avoid doing wrong, and show compassion, just because we know and feel those things ourselves, not under coercion. But people don't seem able to do that.'

'"Compassion" is a lovely word,' she responded. 'I wonder what is its relation to "passion", I mean not just in the grammatical sense. It is lovely, anyway,' tilting her head slightly, smiling in a way that he might almost have thought of as, came close to daring to think of as, affectionately, 'to find someone talking of ideas with such passion, as you have just done. I go months without hearing anyone talking like that.' And in embarrassment he looked around him, through the restaurant that now seemed to have cleared suddenly. Had they been so absorbed? Across at the *Riservato* table he was surprised to see the elderly woman looking directly at him, with something strangely like acknowledgment in her eyes, but of what? Might she, impossibly, have been listening, at such distance? It could only have been a trick of the night. Perhaps it was not him she was looking at at all.

'The rules are so simple, really,' he continued, almost despite himself, the excitement not yet having left him. 'Compassion, avoidance of cruelty, respect for another's being . . . But there are also all sorts of other things, just as fundamental to human being, that get in the way of them, create these paradoxes and collisions. The right to seek one's own comfort. The right to *possess* things. The right to have as much of something as someone else has. Fake rights, cruel rights. There is such ingrained selfishness, such a deeply entrenched self-protectiveness, that turns the eyes, or the heart, or whatever it is that could be the basis of compassion, inward not outward.'

'And love?'

'Love?' He was momentarily confused.

'Yes, as the thing that is the basis of compassion.'

'Well . . . we've been speaking about it all this time in very limited, inward-facing terms, haven't we? As something between individuals, and as something that consumes us, obsesses us. It's an incredibly powerful force, but while it's focused inward like that it's not really doing much good

at all, is it? Apart from the propagation of the species. I mean, it's been wonderful to talk with you,
I have thoroughly enjoyed it – loved it – and I
hope that it can continue for a while longer! But is
it, is this, the real conversation?' He doubted suddenly, wondered whether they were on the right
track at all.

She smiled. As if, he thought, he had at last said
something she had been waiting for.

'Do you mean politics? The human condition? But surely, once lives are saved and crises
averted it is going to be exactly these things that
the conversation turns to, the oldest conversation,
the question of what to do with our lives, how to
conduct them with each other: relationships, love.

'And why, anyway, should it be a matter of one
thing *or* the other?' She wasn't really turning the
conversation away. 'Couldn't it be a matter of one
thing *becoming* the other? As passion, for example,
is at the heart of *com*passion.'

'How do you mean?'

'Maybe the two are in a kind of, what is the
word? symbiosis. Or maybe this human, selfish,
in-facing thing we have been talking about is a
sort of training-ground for something else.'

'The Wheel. If I understand you rightly,' though in truth he was not sure that he did. 'A friend of mine – well, an acquaintance really – once called it the Wheel. An elderly woman, by the time I knew her. A well-known French actress, though not in films, a stage actress.'

'Ah, good,' she said, 'another story! I liked the passion, but I was getting a little bored by the metaphysics.' Humour flashing in her eyes, the mischief back.

'An illustration, of the point you were just making; in fact of the point I think *each* of us was just making, in our different ways.'

'But also a story. A story is a story . . . so go on.'

'I met her while walking my dog. Catherine had a dog too – '

'Catherine? The actress?'

'Yes, Catherine.'

'Deneuve?'

'No, Catherine Deneuve is still very much alive. This Catherine would have been somewhat older, Catherine Dumeny, and has died. That is part of my story.'

'I'm sorry. Continue.'

'She had a dog, a very old dog, a sort of poodle, but it had been crossed with something bigger. A beautiful, large, rangy creature, but old and always tired. It was the dogs that introduced us. We never talked much, and I only ever saw her four or five times in the park, but she always remembered my dog, a kelpie, and we were friendly. She must have been in her mid-seventies. She died about a year after our first conversation, and there were suddenly tributes on television, old interviews, a retrospective.

'I watched one of the interviews. I think she had done it sometime in her sixties. She had had many affairs, apparently, and some famous marriages. I hadn't realised. And she talked at one point about what she called the Wheel, but I suppose others might call it the Rack, of the body and of physical desire. She said that she had been suffering on it – even when it was most deep and exciting she still spoke of it as a kind of suffering – until her late forties or early fifties, when she said it had at last left her.'

'She would also have been speaking about menstruation, and menopause, surely. Menstruation is a rack. For a lot of us the menstrual cycle is the

Wheel of Wheels. And then menopause to follow it! Argh!'

'Yes, of course, certainly, she must have been, though she did not mention them. She said that when the Wheel dropped her – that was her expression, "dropped" – so much had seemed suddenly easier. She became more confident about things, could see the suffering around her more clearly, the suffering of other creatures, and knew better what had to be done. She had *got past herself*, she said, by which I understood that she had got over herself somehow, recovered from a preoccupation with herself. She looked back on her past before that and felt that there had been a lot that had been foolish in it, but also understood herself and what had been happening, and so was not deeply embarrassed. She said that she could see outside herself, in a way she hadn't been able to before.'

'In her late forties, you say? So I have twenty years to go.'

'Yes. I think the interview stayed in my mind because it wasn't long before I was feeling like something similar might be happening to me. Or perhaps I was just hoping. I was happy in the relationship with Genevieve – as I still am, very much so – and something had changed, a restlessness had gone, a looking around me, an unpredictable anxiety, largely sexual, that I only then began to realise had been an albatross on my shoulders from my teens.'

'And this anxiety, this albatross, is gone?'

'The anxiety yes; the interest no.' Did this sound right? how to correct? why did he need to say it? 'But now it's aesthetic, you might say, no longer even very speculative.' Hoping that she would understand his smile. 'It is not that anything has died in me, but the urgency, the obsession, are gone. There is a contentment I'd never expected to feel, at least not in that way. When I *want*, it is my wife I want. I suppose I am very lucky in this. Many men of my age I know, and many women, are not nearly so happy. Some are still lost in their obsessions, at sixty or seventy! I don't suppose the Wheel lets everyone go, or not so early.'

'The actress's dog. What happened to it, I wonder, after she died?'

'I can actually answer that. I saw the notice of her death in the newspaper, with the funeral details, and was tempted to go, but didn't. I looked for a report of it though. It seems her dog was quite famous. I half-expected to read that it had been by the graveside, but apparently it was taken off by a friend, on the day of Catherine's death, and had itself died that night. As if it had known.'

'Of course it knew. A shame that they could not bury it with her.'

'Yes it is, isn't it? She probably would have liked that.'

'And now,' she said, after a pause, 'it is my turn, to go to the Ladies. I won't be long.'

'Shall I order coffee?'

'Yes, please, an espresso.'

'An espresso! I don't think I could handle that myself. Not at this time of night!'

As she moved off he signalled the waiter, ordered, then leant back and looked around him. A large party was leaving the long, shining restaurant on the other side, spilling noisily onto the square. He heard the nearby bell ring once, signalling the half-hour, and wondered what time it was. Half-past ten? Half-past eleven? He had left his watch in the hotel room, remembered it only in the lobby but then reflected with some pleasure that for once he didn't really need it, and so had not gone back up. A day without time. The clock in the tower at the end of the square was supposed to tell the hour dramatically with a march of mechanical figures, but apparently it, too, was not working. Instead he found himself watching a small group drift from the arches near the Tourist Information office and move slowly toward and past him on their way out of the square on the water side. Mother, father, two young children, in bright but worn clothing, harlequinesque, the man tall, lanky, with long hair, a dark, drooping moustache, the woman with a rich red scarf around her head, and large golden earrings. And riding steadily on the man's shoulders, rocking rhythmically back and forth to his gait as one might when riding a horse or camel, clutching his hair like a set of reins, a small monkey, with a green, embroidered cap and jacket. As Stephen watched it turned and watched him, holding his gaze with wide, unblinking eyes as it receded into the darkness, at the very last second baring its teeth – was it a boy? a girl? a shame to think of such a creature as 'it' – in what seemed like a dismissive scowl, but could as likely have been greeting or farewell; he would never know.

He found himself thinking of the conversation, wondering what, as they had followed the twists and turns of it, she had really been thinking. It seemed to him as if he had been as honest as he could, speaking his mind without any . . . what was the word? persiflage? But as so often the more he thought of such questions the more one answer gave way to a deeper one, and a deeper one still. And what of her? He felt, suddenly, in her absence, an old isolation, elemental, like a chill on the night breeze. What was the word he had used before, that had come to him out of nowhere? the shadow? Yes. But probably it was more than that. *Could* it be gendered, something so deep? *Was* it a matter of the sexes? Some profound separation, some ancient conditioning, that left one so uncertain, simply not knowing what another was thinking, was understanding. One had a desire, at last, for absolute honesty, deep, direct communication, yet also this unshakable, nagging feeling that it was no longer possible, if it ever had been. As if you had woken one morning, aching for birdsong, only to realise that you had hunted all the birds. Could he ever hear her, through himself? Could she hear him? Or was it deeper, existential, one human's isolation from another, regardless of gender? Absurdly – he imagined, were he to tell her, that she would only laugh at it – he felt judged somehow, condemned, but of a crime no one would ever discuss with him, no one would ever explain. Was she, this charming younger woman, who seemed to be listening so kindly, exchanging such stories, asking questions as if she truly wanted answers, simply toying with him, experimenting, giving him rope enough to hang himself? No, of course not, a crazy paranoia! So why did he feel it?

'Two-thirds of a cup of flour,' she said, returning with the freshness and strangeness of a wave washing a beach, 'mixed with pinches of dried oregano and salt and coarse-ground black pepper.'

A sign. What else could it be? And he felt the anxiety passing like cloud-shadow, as quickly as it had come.

'Then you mix in a cup of *cold* mineral water, it has to be the kind with gas, and so cold that it is almost frozen. And at the same time you are heating the oil, so hot that it is almost smoking. I used to think it had to be olive oil, but I now think it should be something lighter.'

'The zucchini flowers! The batter!'

'Yes, the zucchini flowers. And then you take the flower – the *male* flower, which has a long, thin stalk – and, holding the stalk, dip it into this mixture then quickly into the oil, which you let froth over it for thirty seconds or so before you turn it over for the same amount of time. And drain it then on a paper towel, and get on with the next and the next. Promise me that you will try!'

'Yes. I promise. I have seen them before in the markets on Edgar Quinet, just never known what to do with them.'

'Did you order the coffee?'

'Yes. Can you tell me the time? Not that it matters, but I heard a bell ring the half-hour, and I was just wondering which.'

'It is ten-forty.'

'Good. The night is still young. I was hoping so.'

'Can I ask you something,' she said, 'a little more personal?'

'A *more* personal question? That should be interesting.'

She smiled and tilted her head slightly. 'I'm sorry. But you seem to have enjoyed talking, and I want to know things!

'You have had a lot of lovers, yes?'

'A lot of lovers? I don't know. How many is a lot? Is there an average?' Defensive. Again.

'How many would you say that you have had?'

'I don't know. I've never counted.'

'Don't play games. Everybody counts them. How many? Forty? Fifty?' She would cajole him, and it was hard to resist her.

'No. Nothing like that. Thirty perhaps. It depends on how you count them, what qualifies someone as a lover.'

'Ah, well, I'll leave that up to you. Thirty, you say?'

'Thirty-three.' He smiled. Relinquishing.

'You see? You have an exact figure!'

'Well then,' they were playing a kind of game now, 'how many have you had?'

'Nine.'

'Your boyfriend, the young one, Paolo; and your teacher; and the Englishman; and the girl on the ship, Graziella; and the person you tested yourself on – '

'And a man while I was living here in Trieste, and another relationship in Torino – none of these very remarkable. And two others.'

'Two others? They sound mysterious.'

'They perhaps don't count. Nothing really happened. Two boys.'

'Two boys?'

'Yes, on the bank of a river, after a party.'

'Two boys on the bank of a river!'

She had started to blush.

'Yes, and nothing happened, and I will not talk about it. You are distracting me from my question.'

'Your more personal question? I thought you had just asked it! And in any case I will not let you escape from your boys so easily. You already owe me a story. You said you would tell me a story, to repay me for mine.'

'But I have told you so many stories!'

'Not as many as I have told you!'

The coffee arrived, and a small silver tray of dark, handmade chocolates, three each.

'Alright, I will tell you about the boys – it is not what you think – but only when you have answered me.'

'Okay then. Ask.'

'You have had affairs, yes?'

'Yes.'

'What was it like?'

'Do you mean all affairs, or do you mean it in the narrower sense, of affairs I had while I was with someone else?'

'The latter, yes.'

'Ah. Thank you. Another easy question. What were they like? Well – '

'No, I mean what was *it* like.' Reaching out for a chocolate. 'Maybe I should say what *is* it like, to *have* an affair. To be betraying someone. How do you feel, as it is happening?'

'I understand,' old regret washing through him, 'and the simple answer is that it is not always very pleasant, but of course that is also misleading, since you don't go into an affair without a certain amount – often a great deal – of excitement and pleasure, much as a lot of that pleasure may be more a kind of instantaneous gratification than an enduring relationship.'

'There have been no enduring relationships, amongst your affairs?'

'I didn't say that. There was once a very endur-ing one. And the others varied. It's not really fair to talk about instantaneous gratification. I had four affairs during my first marriage, to Jane, but to give them all the same name, the same label, doesn't seem right. Even to say that two of them were matters of a kind of momentary, passing desire and that two were relationships doesn't seem right. The relationships were actually love relationships, or something very close; a real infatuation, one of them, intensely sexual, that might have turned into something much longer-lasting had it had a chance, and the other one was a real friendship: with a nun, actually, or a woman who had almost become one, who had left the order at the end of her novitiate. I used to tell myself that if these were all crimes, as part of me felt they were, at least they were all crimes of love. And while I look back on them with regret for my own actions and the way they eventually hurt Jane, it's also with real affection still for those other parties – partners – and a real belief that, wrong as it might have been to have had affairs in the first place, it was perhaps also that I wasn't ready to be married, and that Jane wasn't ready, and that they were, her relationships and my relationships, a kind of process of becoming. That desire was *pulling us through* these things, *leading* us somewhere – and I mean all of us, because you have to remember that an affair is also an intersection, *two* vectors crossing – on a course or courses of its own.'

'Two vectors or three, or four, since that other partner might have a partner, and you have your own partner. A lot of lives to get tangled.'

'Yes, and you can see how it goes. All that making of excuses, all that trying to find angles that put things in a better light.'

'When you probably don't know the real reasons why you are doing it anyway.'

'Yes. And that making of excuses, that you know is a kind of bad faith, erodes you, weakens you in your own eyes. Yet you are pulled. And you never know whether it is a strength or a weakness.'

'Strength? How could you see it as strength?'

'I don't know. To resist ordinariness. To stay alive, vital, when everything around you seems to be deadening you. To go against that tide. There is some restless thing inside you, pushing you.'

'I'm not sure that you can call these things strength. Aren't they just as likely indulgence, weakness? Wouldn't the real strength be to resist these things, or to try to find them within your marriage?'

'Or to end the marriage if it has come to be so bad. But that's what I say: you don't know. You pretend to yourself that it is a kind of strength, and hope that it is, but all along you suspect that it is not. Part of it – I know this may sound strange – is that it's the full weight of conventional wisdom against you, and that wisdom, that convention, seems such a leaden, suffocating thing, almost something you *have* to resist.'

'Surely you could do that in ways that aren't sexual.'

'But that's what I just said, you pretend.'

There was a long pause. As if each of them had come to some sort of obstacle and were trying, mentally, to clamber over it. His an embarrassing pile of old confusions, a dark, tangled wood he'd spent so much energy and emotion trying to find his way through, and regret for damage, the lost time. And hers? Was she applying any of this to her Russian? She seemed to be staring into the base of her empty cup, as if there were something to be read there.

❦

'And the other,' she said eventually, looking up, 'the enduring relationship? That was later? In your second marriage?'

'Yes.'

'So you hadn't *become* very much, had you? I mean by that stage, if it happened again so quickly.'

He could see that she was only partly teasing, was also curious, almost worried, as if starting to chart the ramifications.

'No. It seems in my case that change doesn't happen so quickly. Or didn't, in those days. But this other affair, this enduring relationship, wasn't really so quickly afterward. Eight years, maybe even nine. Something like that. I met Carol three years after that first divorce, and we married a year later. Anne was born the next year, and Simon the year after. Then we moved to Paris.

'The affair I'm talking about, the relationship with Marguerite, began two years after that. She was a work colleague. We got along very well. She had a great sense of humour, and made me feel that I had one also. We laughed a great deal. It's strange to say it but I don't think we would have come together physically if another friend, a male colleague, hadn't said to me one day how beautiful he found her, and how *erotic*. I looked at her differently after that. I hadn't yet seen her that way, but I began to, found myself thinking about her, imagining.'

'Fantasising.'

'Yes, fantasising. And I can't believe that I am talking about this!'

'But you are. And there can be no backing away. We have an agreement. And what, anyway, can be the harm? You will go back to Paris when? You haven't told me.'

'Tuesday.'

'Tuesday! See? In two days. And I will vanish into the night in just another hour or so. This conversation will be a memory, a mirage. So, what happened then, with Marguerite?'

'Nothing, at first. She left. Went to another firm, in a different city. Nothing to do with me. But I missed her much more than I could have imagined. I was surprised. I would even dream of her. And then one day we met in the street quite by accident, near the Panthéon. She was back in Paris for some business. We had a drink at a café nearby, and it was good to be in each other's company once more, so natural. We met again, by arrangement, at a business conference a month later where I think we both knew that we would sleep together. And we did, when we could, for about a year, before she got pregnant, not with my child, but with her husband's – she was married also.

'We stopped, then. I think we invented some excuse, some argument, so that we could be angry with each other, to make it easier. And I went back to my family: I had never left them, of course, not physically, but there's a sense in which your heart does, your mind does. Because you have to live a lie, keep a lot of yourself apart from them. Even the children. Especially them. At that time I remember being so glad that it was over, that I could be whole again, that I could stop lying. I hadn't realised how *divided* I had been. It was like recovering from an illness.'

'But you said "enduring relationship". That is scarcely a year.'

'There is more. We were on holidays on Naxos, in the Cyclades, Carol and the children and I, about two years later. I had pretty much driven Marguerite out of my consciousness. It had been difficult at first, but I think I had been ready for it to finish and so I hadn't *grieved*, as it were. But one morning, on Naxos – we had been very relaxed there, blue water and beaches during the day, and nice meals in the taverna in the evening, and then card-games, some time looking at the stars, sleep, then the same cycle again – one morning I woke up from a dream, a most beautiful dream, in which Marguerite and I were swimming in a deep, sheltered pool among high rock walls, a pool or cove that you could only enter from the sea, through a wide stone arch. We were alone there. The feeling was of absolute, almost unimaginable peace. I woke up and almost immediately was beset by the most profound sadness. I thought at first that Marguerite must have died, and that I had sensed it somehow, but I called her number from a phone in the village, and she answered, so it wasn't that. I hung up immediately, didn't speak with her, but the feeling stayed with me, that I was in the midst of some kind of tragedy, that we had killed something in ourselves and each other. I did not know what to do. Operating on a kind of instinct I sent her a postcard, saying only the truth, that I had had a dream, and woken with a tremendous sadness, and that I could think of nothing to do but to tell her this.

'A couple of weeks after I got back to Paris – I still did not know what to do, but it was much on my mind – I received a phone call from her. She was coming to Paris the next week and wondered if we might meet. I asked her to have lunch with me and, well, it began again, and lasted another two years.'

'How did it end?'

'That's complicated. Her marriage was getting worse. Apparently it had not been good for a long time, but now her husband seemed to resent the child, the daughter.'

'Perhaps because she was yours? *Might* have been yours. Can you ever be sure, without a test?'

'No, she was not mine, *is* not mine, no. I had Marguerite's word on that. And I saw them in Paris at the Gare Montparnasse a couple of years ago – they did not see me – and while the resemblance between them was striking, there was no resemblance whatsoever to me. But I said it was complicated and I am coming to that.'

'Still.'

'Still. And eventually the husband left – left

both her and the daughter. He came home one night, with another woman, and confronted Marguerite, said that he was going to move out, to live with her. And things changed, then, between Marguerite and me. The structure of things. We had each had partners. We had *each* been having this affair, which was, in a way, mutually supportive, helped us go on with our separate marriages, and allowed us to be and to stay *lovers*, if you know what I mean. But now one of us didn't, *she* didn't, and her needs, her desires for the relationship changed, were now different from mine. She wanted a permanent relationship, wanted me to leave Carol, and suddenly I realised that I didn't want to do that, that that was not what it had been about. I had thought our relationship was different. It *was* different, or had been – we had talked about it many times! But now something in that arrangement had become exposed. *I* felt exposed. And I guess I fled. It was like finding oneself standing suddenly at the edge of an abyss. I saw the huge damage I was being asked to do. It seemed, suddenly, as if I was about to lose everything. My children, my wife, my house, my reputation, everything. And I fled. Ignominious. Not one of the proudest moments of my life.'

The waiter appeared, asked if they would like anything else, a cognac? Amaretto? No, but realising that it was time, he asked for the bill.

'Is that what affairs are about?' She seemed slightly disappointed, as if she had been hoping for a different story. 'I suppose it is. I have never been married, but I suppose marriage changes things. You must slip away from being lovers, become too familiar and accustomed, and yet I suppose part of you still continues to want the lover who was the beginning of the relationship in the first place. When you look toward someone else it is a lover you want, not a partner.'

'Yes, that's part of it. You wake up sometime and you miss that intensity. It burns inside you, smoulders. A lot of marriages don't seem to have that problem. Perhaps in some cases because there wasn't that sort of intensity in the first place. A lot of people who condemn affairs maybe don't understand this.'

'Is that how you eventually justified your affairs? Is that what you told yourself?'

'I've said that those earlier affairs, in the first marriage, were different. Immaturities, explorations, in a relationship that wasn't ready or perhaps strong enough. If you remove the word "marriage" from that situation, take away the ambiguous fact of it, they begin to look a little more like they were. Probably a great many unmarried people would have had that number of relationships, or more, over such a period of time and at that stage in their lives. But with Marguerite? Yes, I guess I did tell myself that. I told myself a lot of things, made a lot of excuses about myself, to myself. And where there are multiple excuses it probably just means that none of them is right. Later I thought of them as the mind once again trying to justify something – you know, the body, desire, their own mysterious laws – that it was inadequate to deal with.'

'What were some of those things that you told yourself? How *did* you try to justify it?'

Before he could answer the bill arrived, as if to rescue him. He opened the folder, looked at it, stalling for time, and was surprised to find that it was for his meal alone. She was smiling when he looked up, as if she had been right about something. 'I paid for mine inside,' she said, 'since I knew that you would want to pay for me. I thought it would save us one of those silly discussions. But thank you for the thought.' He slid his credit card into the folder, left it on the corner of the table. At some point it slipped away.

'Well,' she persisted, 'what *were* your justifications?'

'I have done so much talking. You must be sick of it. And they are, I don't know, complicated, inadequate, stupid.' Suddenly he felt that it was all indefensible, had always been so. That nothing excused the damage. That trying to explain himself, the person he was back then, was beyond him.

'Human, probably, more than anything,' she was rescuing him again. 'And if I were sick of it, as you put it, I would not be asking for more. I told you, you are twice my age, at least that, and I am taking advantage of you, of your experience, as a male. I need to know. I have never had this opportunity before! It is not as if my father would ever talk to me like this!'

'But I have been just as interested in you, and to waste the conversation by filling it with my own voice – '

'You said yourself that conversations were sometimes about hearing your own voice, hearing what you say, because a lot of things come out that you might not have thought about in the same way otherwise. And you also say that you cannot believe that you are talking about such things. So, by your own definitions, even you might be getting something out of this.'

'What? Reminders of my own stupidities? Yes, okay, but – '

The waiter returned with the credit-slip for signature. He added a generous tip, signed, handed it back, and looked across to find her standing, gathering her book and her bag.

'A walk,' she said, much to his relief. 'Down by the water. There is still much that you are going to tell me.'

He stood, reached for his jacket, and, thanking the waiter as they passed him, followed her carefully through the tables toward the potted olive trees that marked the restaurant's outer entrance, across which, at that moment, darted a large white cat, black-collared. The same, yes, heading for a dark doorway off to the left. And when they issued into the dimness of the square, cued somehow, her spell again? the fountain began. They walked over and stood by it, watching the bright water as it formed a dark pool. As if to reward their interest, a light in the water flickered and came on and then, a whole system seemingly taking its cue, a thousand blue paving lights he'd not noticed before sprang into life, like ranks of dominoes falling, and the entire piazza was transformed.

'Magical,' she said. 'I'd heard about this but hadn't seen it. They put the lights in after I left. I thought they would be terrible, but this is good, wonderful, like walking on water!'

MOLO

She took his arm, but it was only so as to lead him off across the wide square, and to begin their conversation again.

'So,' she said, walking slowly, looking across to him, 'what were these stories, these excuses you gave yourself?'

'Haven't I been telling you?'

'No, not really. I sense that there are excuses behind the excuses, and that we have not got to them yet. I need to know. And how often am I going to have a captive source?'

'Captive?' But yes, it did feel like that. A willing captive, being led toward the dark water, over the shining stones.

'Maybe the most stupid was the sense that it

was a kind of French thing – that there was more acceptance of affairs and infidelities in France, a kind of cultural acceptance.'

'That's certainly the impression you get, from the books and the films, that France is more liberated that way.'

'Yes, but I think, after living so long there, that it's a cruel liberation, if it's a liberation at all, one that may suit the men but that tends rather to bully the women.'

'"Bully" them?'

'You know, force them, coerce them somehow. I am always, every day, surprised at how patriarchal a society France is. It's so old and so deeply entrenched that there's a whole labyrinth of disguises and excuses that covers it up, but the official, cultural, public acceptance masks a lot of private suffering. I've never known a place where *scent* is so important, *clothes* are so important, *fashion* is so important – where women are expected to spend so much of their lives trying to appeal to and servicing the desires of men, are deprived of so much of their own time and their own mental space because of it.'

'That's very Italian, too. I suppose that is all part of the *economy* you were talking about. But still you told yourself, at first, that this somehow made your affair more acceptable.'

'Yes, I tried the idea, but probably more because it was convenient. I only half-believed it, if I believed it at all. I was so *aware*, you know – this is shameful, an embarrassment to say – of the *certain* hurt and damage there would be to Carol if she learnt about Marguerite, and of how pathetic and untrue it was to think that she was just, you know, not *French* enough. If anything, being Australian just meant that she wasn't pre-supplied with a whole lot of repressive self-deceptions about it.'

'Yet you had the affair anyway. So what else were you telling yourself? What,' she was smiling, 'was the next most stupid thing?'

'The interesting thing about having an affair with someone who is also married is that while you are trying to explain yourself to yourself, you are also able to listen to them doing so, as if you were looking into a kind of mirror. For a start – and I don't think I'm being defensive here – it reminds you of something that is often overlooked when people talk about such things: that affairs, if they are heterosexual, it goes without saying, are between a man and a woman. That it is not just the man who is doing something to the woman he betrays, but that another woman is a part of it, is doing something to the man *she* betrays.'

'Obviously, though I can't see that it wouldn't be the same if they were homosexual affairs or lesbian affairs: surely the same deception and betrayal are involved. And it seems to take us back to where we started. That's part of my problem, after all. I know that it is in a sense up to me to decide whether I am prepared to do this to Andrei's wife.'

'So that is his name? Your Russian?'

'Yes, Andrei. I didn't tell you? But you were speaking of your mirror. What did you see in it?'

'Only that we each tried to blame our partners somehow. Each of us was acutely aware of that old excuse that your wife – husband, in Marguerite's case – doesn't understand you, but we fell into the trap anyway; slowly, subtly started to find fault with Carol on my side, Pierre-Marie on hers. Carol was a little cold and awkward with me sexually, she always had been, and I blamed her for that, for an intimacy and physical affection that she had always had trouble showing, whereas Marguerite was so open and generous. And for Marguerite it was similar: something she had seen at first as a disarming shyness in Pierre-Marie, emotionally, that had challenged and even excited her, had come to seem a coldness, an inability to respond. She complained about his long working hours, the time he spent at the gym, his obsession with his car, and I complained – when I say "complained" I am not really saying that we talked about these things very much; it's more what we were telling ourselves, but it would seep out – about Carol's coldness. But, you know, when Pierre-Marie revealed that he had been having an affair himself it became clear to me – not so readily to Marguerite – that he might have found someone he was *not* so cold with, and that the coldness might not have been so much in him as in their relationship somehow, a sort of chemical mismatch that hadn't been evident at the start, but that had emerged as time had passed. And seeing that in *her* marriage got me to see that it might have been similar in my own. They're all *relationships* after all; people *in relation*, as we've said. But it's so hard to see outside yourself sometimes. Even when you think you are doing so most clearly. Perhaps especially then. We have such amazing powers of self-deception.'

They had reached the waterfront. The Molo Audace. Hadn't there been a *mole* somewhere, in *The French Lieutenant's Woman*? A long stone pier? Certainly this one – broad, angular, paved with huge squares of, what, basalt? – seemed, *audacious*, to go on for miles, could have been a landing-strip. They found, after two or three minutes strolling in silence into the sea breeze, distracted by the sensuous feel of it as it brushed them, almost like a tepid, rarefied water on their face, a wooden bench and sat with their backs to the sea, looking at the huge square and the lights of the city behind it. Irena was right, the blue paving lights made the piazza seem awash, if one were prepared to imagine this black, lapping, whispering water could thin to such a soft lightness.

'The Piazza Unità,' he said, not unintentionally changing the subject, 'for the unification of Italy? I'm surprised there's no statue of Garibaldi, or of Victor Emmanuel.'

'It's not *that* unification. The name of the piazza has gone back and forth. Like a conversation, as I once heard someone say. It was all explained very carefully to me when I first came here. It was originally the Piazza San Pietro – there was once a church there, in the centre, I think – then it became the Piazza Grande, and was called that all through the nineteenth century. It only became the Piazza Unità with the reunification of Trieste with Italy in 1918. Then – I cannot remember when, but some time later – it became Piazza Francesco Giuseppe, and then when the city was again reunited with Italy, after the brief occupation by Tito and the period of American and British administration, it was made the Piazza Unità again.'

'Sounds more like a battle than an argument or a conversation. Who was Francesco Giuseppe?'

'The Emperor Franz Joseph! This whole area was under Austrian domination right up until the end of World War I.'

'Ah. I guess I should have worked that out. So why call it Piazza Francesco Giuseppe after that?'

'I don't know. Nostalgia maybe: the region was in such dispute through most of the twentieth century, and there had at least been stability under the Austrians. But I really have no idea.'

'And the Molo Audace? It is called that because it is so huge?'

'*Ow-dá-chay*,' she said, correcting him. 'No.

The *Audace* was the first ship from the Italian Navy to enter the port after the reunification in 1918.'

'Audacious . . .' He would have resisted the term *inebriated*, but there was a warmth, through the veins, that did not seem to stop at his finger-tips, and he was still smarting, not unpleasantly, from the lesson in pronunciation.

A motor-launch passed forty or fifty metres off-shore, its bow-waves rocking the moored fleet of dinghies and motorboats nearby, producing a jingling of chains and tackle that, even after the sound of the motor had faded, continued down the anchorage toward the distant railway station. Gulls wheeled above them. Night gulls. There would be fish nosing the prows. That octopus somewhere. Dark out here. Moon obscured by cloud. When had that come in?

'What other excuses did you offer to yourself? You did say there were several.'

'Ah. I thought I might have escaped at last.'

'Not at all. You are still in the net. Though I'm hoping the next excuses are better.'

'Well, there *was* another, I suppose no more nor less foolish than the rest. That there was a kind of need or drive in me that others wouldn't understand. A restlessness.'

'The Wheel?'

'Yes, but also different, something more. That there are some people who are *lovers* – almost as if they were a different species – and others, the great majority, who are not. But we've already talked about this. I began to think that it was something about society, and about its outcasts. What society cuts off – excludes – of a kind of wider being in us. I even read Freud, trying to think through this: *Beyond the Pleasure Principle*, and *Civilization and its Discontents . . .'*

'So you blamed the whole civilisation? That is a little – what is the word? – megalomaniac? *audacious*?' He could hear the smile in her voice.

'Megalomaniacal? Perhaps. It's certainly narcissistic. But I don't really think that's what I was doing, and there were some interesting thoughts that came from it. I also read a book – I'd seen a review of it in a newspaper and wanted to know what the man's reasoning was – about a novelist, a famous Czech novelist, who had had many affairs and several marriages and who had argued that he needed the sexual excitement of new relationships for his creativity, that there was some inherent connection between sexuality and creativity. He seemed incapable of exploring and explaining this, took it as some sort of mystery, but although you have called me a mystic I am in fact suspicious of mysteries. And I had this idea that, if there *was* any kind of connection, it must be in the guilt of it, the shame of it, to one-self: I don't mean if you are found out, if you are exposed, but the guilt you must feel – the guilt I *did* feel – and the way it made you try to explain yourself to yourself, so that your understanding would increase, you would discover things about yourself and your motivation, and about society, about values, about good and evil, maybe even about thought itself.'

'So, you thought that having an affair might make you wiser? A better electrical engineer?' The thought, when she put it so directly, seemed sud-denly so bizarre that he burst out laughing, and she, too, after a second, out on the dark mole.

'No,' he said eventually, 'I don't think I ever applied it to myself, not that way.'

'I was a bit unfair too. But it sounded so stupid, the way you put it, that – '

'Stupid! Thank you!' But it was play, not real alarm.

'No, not that you were saying it stupidly, but that you put it so clearly that the stupidity of it became suddenly very apparent. And as I was just saying, it's a bit unfair for me to dismiss it completely. But it's just another instance of the artist's use of the female muse, yes? This book, *Possession*, is full of this, I think. And it may be that the muse is so fascinating to the artist because, in a patriarchal society, so much is repressed along with the feminine that the feminine *is* a kind of channel to the thoughts and ideas that the society won't allow. And, if you're an artist, if you get tired of one affair – if the relationship loses its eroticism, becomes too familiar, too domesticated – I suppose you might well think you needed another. So, you see, I do admit that there might be a connection between desire and thought, sexuality and thought, and so between affairs and thought. But surely it's more a symptom of a disease than anything very intelligent in itself. I certainly don't think it helps with building concrete plants or medical facilities.'

※

'And? Is that all? The explanations you were offering yourself?'

She would keep pushing. And if some part of him wished there were some way of stalling, another more masochistic one was relishing the process, determined to shock or revolt, or perhaps it was just to embarrass and humiliate itself, before this strange girl the age of one of his daughters. Was it perhaps *them* he was confessing to? Could he ever talk to one of them like this? Marina perhaps. Anne probably never, his longest and most complexly beloved, to whom he'd have most liked to be able to explain. And be absolved by? Was that it, to be absolved?

'Well, no. There's another. I used to wonder, too, whether I might be punishing myself, whether it might all be part of some deeper drama.'

'Deeper?'

'I was risking everything. And I knew I was. I would sometimes reel at the thought of it. A sort of chill would shoot through me. A terror. Of losing my children, of losing a wife whom I loved, for certainly I thought I did, and *did*, love Carol: it *is* possible to love two people. And of losing my sense of self, too, shattering my sense of myself as you might shatter a mirror, showing my falseness, some sort of quintessential falseness, to the world but especially to myself. Losing everything. A kind of dissolution, of death. And yet I would go on, *knowing* – for believe me I *did* know, *did* recognise its inevitability – that I would get caught, that the affair would be known. As if I wanted, in some part of me, to lose everything, everything and everyone I loved. Wanted that punishment some-how, wanted that sort of death; was using that love, that affair, to commit a bizarre kind of suicide.'

'Eros and thanatos,' she said, cautious and quiet, as if her mind had just stepped back, in the presence of something.

'I know,' he said, 'that oldest connection. And I've thought about it. But it doesn't *explain* any-thing. Or rather it does, but in a way that just leaves you wanting so much more. In some ways it is just there, as if you'd wandered into a myth. But perhaps the myth is there in the first place just to give a kind of comforting story to something that keeps happening to humans that they *can't* explain.

'And of course it is also what happened, in a way. There was a crisis, in my relationship with Marguerite. She had given me a kind of ultimatum.

I handled it badly. But perhaps it was also time. And I told Carol about her.

'Even in my worst envisionings I couldn't have imagined the rage and the horror and the hurt it caused. We argued furiously for six months. For a time I did not see Marguerite at all, did not want to, since it seemed to me that I was forced to deny her – betray her – so often, and when she found me, came to me at last in confusion, I asked her for time to try to sort things out with Carol. And then she, too, Marguerite, was enraged and heart-broken. She left me that day saying that she never wanted to see me again. I had lost her, and within a few more months Carol had returned to Australia with the children and I had lost them also. But that's where this conversation began. The divorce. We've come a big circle.'

'And then?'

'Four years, then, of loneliness and self-disgust and regret, and the constant fantasy that I could repair things with Marguerite, for it was she whom I dreamt of, and who wouldn't leave my subconscious, for the longest time. But she had vanished. I could have tried to trace her – I did, once or twice, begin – but in my self-loathing I didn't see how I could impose myself on her even if I found her and she could forgive me. It was fairly clear, anyway, that she wouldn't vanish without trace if she herself had any such fantasy.'

'Even if she had, and you had come together again, it would have been hard for her to trust you.'

'Yes, and would have been based upon brokenness, built over scar tissue. And it *was* a bit like that, you know? A sudden *accident*. As if you were driving along a highway and then suddenly something had happened, you had veered, hit something, and there were people trapped in the wreckage, people in intensive care, taking years to rehabilitate. My children have come back to me: a kind of grace from them that I can't pretend to deserve, but even with them there was, for the longest time, a bruisedness, I was going to say a tenderness, as in soreness, after a strain or something, not the other kind of tenderness, but perhaps tenderness is the right word after all.

'It's strange, how no one ever tells you about these things, from the inside. There is always the folk-wisdom, the social wisdom. I rather resent, even now, the kind of smugness I used to imagine on society's face, as if to say, We told you all along.

It's not just the smugness and hypocrisy, though they are there in almost every direction you look. It's the half-living, half-knowing it's based upon. Inheriting the rules, living by them. I still feel something is being shut out by that, being repressed by it. As if these two things – love and desire on the one side and society on the other – were somehow at loggerheads. I still insist there's a pearl in this oyster, a solution, a secret, even if I haven't been able to find it yet, unless it's Genevieve herself and I suppose it is. But how to explain that? That after all this wrongness and stupidity I should end up so happy, in the strongest and calmest relationship of my life? I have to admit to you that that *is* a mystery.'

'"Loggerheads"? I've come across it, but have never understood the term.'

'Things locked together in dispute, stubborn, irresolvable. Another Gordian knot. But also, in another sense, a kind of opposite of that. I think it's amazing, you know, how almost every day you can find in the newspapers a story of someone in a high position – a president, a government minister, an archbishop, some top businessman, a head of the police – caught out for something sexual as if they've been all along on the same collision course, risking everything for some uncontrolled and probably uncontrollable desire, or people just turning their backs on all they've done, all they've built up, because the way that they feel for someone they've met just suddenly outweighs everything. Some of the highest things, supposedly, in human terms, political success, financial success, intellectual success, spiritual accomplishment, brought back to that.

'Love, tenderness . . .' he might now have been speaking in a trance, 'are the most dangerous capacities we have, I sometimes think. The dark places they open and expose, the gulfs, as if love – even these tentative beginnings, these minor forms, all this pettiness – backs onto, is only the beginning of extinction, as if we desire our own destruction, thinking only that we are desiring one another,' thinking of the hot passage of seed, the life concentrated in it, and the death. Ecstasy. Disease. Elixir and poison at once. Lives, thrown away, so that it, the seed, could be placed in a particular person, or be received from a particular person – so that the *ovum* could receive.

'Well, it is called the Little Death, isn't it? Ejaculation, orgasm. A dying while we are still very much alive. Perhaps the expression registers more than we know, though it might be more of a male perception than a female one, despite the myth. I must admit that it has never seemed much like a dying to me. I grant it can be annoying when it stops. But then', smiling, 'perhaps women have more resources.'

A gust of wind? No, but a stronger breeze, the edge of something, seemed to pull him back to himself. Tiredness, probably. And then silence. Someone had spoken to him, once, about the Angel of Silence, hovering over a room. Could it hover over a harbour, a city? Evidently not. Now that he listened for it there was sound everywhere, muted but constant. The bell, for example, ringing the half-hour again. Eleven-thirty. And the sound of gulls, the soft clink of chains, strain of ropes, rustle of water, late traffic. He was tired, had talked too much, no matter what she said, no matter how kind she was about it. No matter how much she might have wanted to hear.

'Would you like another coffee somewhere?' This was her now.

'No, no. It is lovely out here. The breeze is just the right temperature. Let's stay for a while longer. Another coffee and I wouldn't be able to sleep.'

'Good, but I thought I should offer, you know, to keep your strength up, for all these questions.'

'My strength is fine,' not doubting it, but longing for quietness. 'Tonight, especially.'

'Tell me how you met Genevieve.'

'It was funny. So ordinary. A supermarket trolley. You know how children like to be in charge of them? A young girl was trying to manoeuvre this trolley, and was having a hard time of it because the trolley was so heavy. And my foot was just in the wrong place at the wrong time. I could see it coming, you know, but had my arms full, couldn't see where to put my feet. By the onions, in the fruit and vegetable section. The girl was distraught, and her mother also, and the supermarket management was so afraid I would sue. We had to fill in forms, and I had to sign an indemnity, while in agony! They tried to get me to say that it was the mother's fault for not supervising the child properly, but I had had children and could still remember how hard and unpredictable supervising them can be, so I refused to blame the mother, said they could only have their indemnity if I could ensure it for the mother as well. I hobbled out of there in such pain that all I could think of doing was getting back to my apartment. I went to the hospital the next day and had an X-ray and found that I had broken two of the longish bones in the top of the foot, two tarsal bones. I had to have the foot in plaster. I was lurching along the street on crutches a week later and I met them, the mother and daughter, and they were so concerned and embarrassed. The daughter started to cry. And the mother insisted on having my address, and on bringing me dinner. They did it almost every night until the cast was off, and by that stage, it was weeks later, we were almost a family. It was summer and they had even changed their holiday plans so that they could look after my foot. When the cast came off we went on a holiday together. Genevieve and I became lovers in the holiday house at the beach. I had been deeply attracted to her from almost the moment I saw her. And it was with Marina's blessing. She practically opened champagne. I think I was the first real father figure she had had. And in the ten years since then – she was seven when she ran over me – we have become so close that she might have been my own daughter all along.'

'What had happened to her actual father?'

'He'd tried to persuade Genevieve to have her aborted, and Genevieve had slammed the door on him, quite literally. He was one of those cases I was speaking about a little while ago. A senior minister in the French government. Genevieve had been his mistress for six years, ever since her third year in university. He'd set her up in an apartment – actually *bought* it for her, put it in her name. And when she got pregnant he blamed her, said that she was trying to manipulate him, and insisted that she have an abortion. She refused. And in the argument that followed he'd hit her – the way she tells it it's fairly clear that he was trying to bring on a miscarriage. And when he left she locked the door on him quite literally. Had the locks changed. Let it be known to him that if he ever came back she would reveal much more than the punch. And he stayed away. He was married, of course, but it wasn't just that. Who knows? It's France and he might even have been more popular had it been revealed that he had a beautiful young mistress. But no, he just went silent, disappeared from Genevieve's life. The only explanation she can come up with is that the money he had used to buy the apartment was not entirely his own, or that there was something else about the situation that would have undone him if it were revealed. She'd always had this hunch about it, the way he'd so readily put the apartment in her name.'

'It could have been generosity, or love.'

'Yes, I suppose it's possible, though it's hard to reconcile that with the punch in the stomach.'

'Does Marina know who her real father is?'

'Was. He was killed in a car crash when she was four. On the autoroute south of Paris. Lost control of his Porsche in wet weather. A horrible thing. There were photographs in all the newspapers. I remember them myself. But ironically it made it a lot easier on Genevieve. She could be honest without repercussions – you know, if Marina had eventually wanted to meet her father, to confront him. There's a sort of grace in it all. She doesn't have to know that he wanted her aborted. I suppose she could confront his family, but I doubt she'll do that. She's very well balanced, independent, not the kind for recriminations, doesn't think the world owes her anything.'

They paused, turning to watch the dark harbour and the lights of the ships riding at anchor. From behind them the same bell he had heard before began to strike the hour and he counted. Nine. Ten. Eleven. Twelve. And as soon as it stopped another, further off, began. Lest there be any doubt.

'Midnight,' she said. 'It is time for me to drive you to your hotel. I am sorry to say.'

'Yes. I am sorry too. This has been wonderful, a memorable evening. But there is no need to drive me. I can get a taxi. There was a full rank of them back by the piazza.'

'I am not thinking about need, I am thinking about my own pleasure,' she said. 'Driving is so beautiful on a night like this, when you can have the window down.'

'But it's twenty kilometres each way!'

'Where is it?'

'About seven or eight kilometres on this side of Monfalcone, on the Strada Costiera, a little before Sistiana.'

'Then that decides the matter! You cannot even argue that it is very much out of my way since Claudia's apartment is already seven kilometres in that direction. My car is in the parking lot just over here.' She was already standing, waiting for him to start out with her.

'Very well then, yes, and with pleasure, to continue the talk,' although for the time being they walked almost wordlessly the hundred metres back along the mole and then another hundred through the thinning ranks of dark cars between the Piazza Unità and the Canal Grande, stopping eventually at a small, late-model black Fiat whose lights had just signalled to them.

'That woman,' she paused before opening the car door, looking across the roof to him, 'the one on the beach. Where were the rocks that her husband was washed from?'

'She'd led us, my friend and I, to believe they were further down the coast, but the first time the police questioned me it became clear that they had been the rocks right there, at the foot of the cliff, directly below the house.'

'So sad.'

'Yes,' he said, and watched the night for a moment. A snow-white cat flashed across the dark bitumen – catapulted – between the rows of nearby cars. Heading for the Molo? Rats out there? Or just to see him off. Gone almost before he had noticed it. Invisible now. Strange, the friends one makes, remembering the cat's fur, its raised chin, the feel of its tongue on his thumb. He smiled, got in, closed the door behind him, inhaled, luxuriously, the interior, a mix of new car smell and something else, her scent. Not perfume. Her.

They drove off in silence, past the railway station and through the streets of the city and the cool breath of their tall, dark plane-trees. By the time they had reached the more open road, the veil of cloud he had noticed while they were on the Molo had drifted eastward and very shortly, on the Viale Miramare, they found themselves driving directly toward a large moon, almost at the full, setting over the sea to the west. After what must have been five or six kilometres of long, dark beach they drove briefly through forest and there was the rich, moist smell of fern before they broke out into the open night again, but higher now, the road a ribbon cut into the mountainside. He found himself staring at the sharp outline of a cliff-top castle, the moon beyond it bathing its turrets in liquid silver and creating, over the black water below, a long, gleaming pathway. On the stereo a woman was singing a dark blue ballad – there was no other way to describe it – accompanied by what seemed to be cellos, a lute, a classical guitar, a piece full of night, deep water and longing, in a language he did not understand. Spanish, he thought at first, but it wasn't that. Portuguese? The four things – moon, castle, music, and the vast panorama of the night – seemed to have suddenly come together. He must have gasped, or perhaps just moaned slightly, in appreciation.

'Yes, Castello Miramare. Beautiful, isn't it? Have you been there?'

'No. I looked for it this morning, from the other side. They have postcards at the hotel. But the taxi-driver said – '

'Do you know the story?' interrupting, but it hardly mattered: the castle, high over the moon's path, mantled in liquid light, was already something out of a different, more tenebrous reality, a folktale, an operatic dream.

'Story? No.'

'It was built by Archduke Maximilian of Austria, the brother of Emperor Franz Joseph, for his wife, Charlotte of Belgium, the daughter of Leopold I.'

'One of the most evil men of the nineteenth century.'

'Really? I didn't know. How do you mean?'

'He masterminded the conquest and exploitation of the Congo, in effect a kind of genocide.'

'You mean Leopold II, his son – Charlotte's brother.'

'Sorry. You're quite correct, now that I think about it – ' after a momentary confusion, but there had been a strange lurch toward something, a glimpse of an abyss that their conversation – all night? – had been hanging over. 'I have mistaken the father for the son. So go on, tell me. Please.'

'She was very young. I think maybe sixteen or seventeen, and he was not much older, twenty-five at the most. His brother appointed him governor here. They lived in the little *castelletto* while the bigger castle was being built. But not for very long. Maximilian and Charlotte were asked to become the first Emperor and Empress of Mexico. They renounced all their European titles – and there were probably quite a few, since everyone seemed related to everyone, as if almost all of Europe's rulers were from the one large family – but within a very few years, three or four, all their European relatives had abandoned them to their Mexican empire, which was on the verge of being taken over by the Mexicans themselves.'

'If only that could have happened in the Congo.'

'Charlotte came back by herself to beg desperately for help from the Austrians and the French and others, even the Pope, but everyone turned their back on her. I think they all realised that it was a lost cause. And she had a breakdown and was eventually declared insane. And in Mexico, at almost exactly the same time, Maximilian was executed by the new government. By firing squad. There is a famous painting of that, by Goya I think. Charlotte lived for a long time afterward, waiting for Maximilian to come back to her.'

'And they only lived in Miramare for a few years?'

'Yes, three or four, before the world opened up and sucked them in.'

'You seem to have studied them.'

'No, not really. But their love is a kind of local legend, and I did read a book about them. It was trying to complicate the story. It claimed that she had an affair just after he died, had an illegitimate child, that Maximilian had been impotent, or perhaps just not interested. Who knows what the truth is?'

'At least I know now where the name of my hotel comes from.'

'Really? What is it?'

'The Albergo Villa Carlotta. Perhaps her ghost haunts the place.'

'I doubt it. She came back here for a little while but then went back to Belgium, didn't stir much from there for the next sixty years. But probably she and Maximilian made love, while they were here, looking out over this sea.'

'Probably. The sea doesn't change that much. And if not them then millions of others have made love here and looked out over it.' The air through the open window was soporific, like velvet, coasting his fingers. She lit a cigarette, blew the smoke out into the night.

'The boys!' he said suddenly, remembering: 'You promised to tell me about the boys on the riverbank.'

'I was hoping you had forgotten them. But yes, alright, although now I am afraid I will only disappoint you. Nothing actually happened on the riverbank at all. It was just a moment, a situation.'

'A moment? How do you mean?'

'One of those things one realises, about desire, or maybe just about one's own desire. I was at university, in Padua, and there was a weekend party out in the country, in a house on the river. Two boys were in love with me and I was in love with both of them, for different reasons. Very confused. And they were best friends. We had a difficult few days. I slept with one of them – it is just the way things developed at the time – and the other lay awake in another room all night, wracked by desire and jealousy. I knew how he would be feeling. I went to him, at five in the morning, and we went out to walk since we couldn't talk where we were. We made a kind of nest in the long, wet grass and I held him, and we cried together. I really felt as if I was being pulled in two. And later that day, in the sunshine, in the afternoon, the three of us sat on the riverbank. One of them on one side of me and the other on the other. Something had relaxed – we were emotionally exhausted – and for a little while there was peace. But I can never remember a time, a moment, that was so full of desire.'

'What were they like, these boys? Were they so similar?'

'Similar! No! It seemed at the time that they

could not have been more different. One of them was a blond boy from a rich family in the city, the other a dark-haired boy from a poor farming family, and each of them quite brilliant but, what is your expression, one of them born with a spoon in his mouth?'

'Silver, with a silver spoon.'

'Yes, and the other with salt, and salt can make you so thirsty. I met the other one first, the silver one, and we were lovers for a while, and I thought I was in love with him, and he had introduced me to his friend. I was attracted, very attracted. He was thirsty, you know, in every way, unpredictable, demanding, dangerous, even as a lover, so strong, so hard, so *urgent*, so beautiful. And everything, even his skin, even his semen tasted of salt.'

'And you loved him.'

'Oh yes.'

'And what happened?'

'He was killed in a motorcycle accident, a year later. There were two of them killed, he and his passenger, a girl.'

'And that is why you didn't want to tell me.'

'Yes.'

They drove on in silence. Laced with that haunting music, turned down so that they had been able to talk, but still there, entwined with the breeze from her open window. In the racing dark his mind wandered. A microsleep. A waking dream. He had been thinking of the young boy, his stiff penis arching, hot seed bursting into her: and a hot, answering wetness, swallowing. Her? Genevieve?

'So, Signor Mitchell!' – his name shocked him. How long had they been silent, seconds? minutes?

'Your hotel, the Albergo Villa Carlotta,' and she brought the car to a stop opposite its dimly lit entrance, looking out as she did so as if searching for him already in one of the windows above. He was disappointed at how quickly they had arrived, would have delayed this moment an hour or more if he could.

They sat for several seconds not speaking, as if each were separately thinking what next should be said. After such conversation, what last words could there be? It raced through his mind that he knew so little about her, did not have her address, her phone number, but how now to ask without disturbing something, breaking a spell? Let it be.

Almost unthinking then, since it seemed like

the right thing to do – they had had such a pleasant evening, such a long conversation, had become so much like friends – and saying goodnight as he did so, he leant over toward her, in the dark car, to touch his cheek to hers, kiss the air beside her, and moved to do the same on the other side, to find, as he did so, the faint brush of open lips, and feel the surge of himself, into that encounter, the warmth, the hint of smoke as his eyes closed and he gave himself to it, the thought of what it was that he was doing, as he sank into this long, blind moment, like a distant shout, from a shore somewhere, out by the moon's path.

He pulled away, gently and reluctantly, and tried to read her eyes in the faint light. They seemed to implore, but whether to kiss her again, to stay, to go, to say nothing, he couldn't tell. She leant toward him, pulled him to her and kissed him once more, as long and deep, even longer, then broke from him, pushed him lightly but firmly away. He whispered goodnight again, heard her do the same, then opened the door, gathered his jacket from the back seat and, hearing the door close behind him, walked slowly toward the hotel entrance – could feel her, as he did so, watching, not yet starting the car, not yet moving off. At the top of the three stone steps, not able to stop himself, he turned, about to say something, about to wave, the heart turning almost physically in his chest. But there was nothing. Nothing. No car, no lights moving away, no traffic, as far as the eye could see, anywhere on the long, straight road. Only an old man on a bicycle riding slowly toward Monfalcone, a little the worse for wear to judge by his swaying, his rear wheel scraping rhythmically against the dry mudguard, while a wire rapped against one of the empty flagpoles and an awning, Robbie's, flapped in the stiffening breeze.

Acknowledgments

The author wishes to thank Judith Lukin-Amundsen yet again for her editing, and Tim Curnow, Bert Pribac, Tatiana Stoltenberg, Sergei Androv, Camilla Edgewood, Anna Paglia and, most particularly, Teja Pribac, for their support, encouragement and contributions.